To Omri

Best wis

Jonn

CRISPS

J onny Zucker is an award-winning author with
over 100 books to his name. He writes for all ages,
from picture books to YA fiction. His work has been
translated into 25 languages and his books have sold
over 1 million copies worldwide. His series have included *Monster Swap* (the first book was a Richard
& Judy Summer Children's Book Club Read), *Striker
Boy* (Shortlisted and long listed for 6 awards) and
Max Flash. He is in the top 10% of library-borrowed
children's authors in the UK. He was the writing
consultant on BBC 2's *Gareth Malone's Extraordinary
School for Boys*. Along the way he has tried his hand
at primary school teaching, football coaching and
stand-up comedy. He is crazy about crisps (the
snack) and had enormous fun writing this book.

CRISPS

JONNY ZUCKER

THREE HARES PUBLISHING

Published by Three Hares Publishing 2015

First published in Great Britain in 2015
www.threeharespublishing.com

Three Hares Publishing Ltd Reg. No 8531198
Registered address: Suite 201, Berkshire House, 39-51 High Street,
Ascot, Berkshire, SL5 7HY

ISBN 9781910153147

Printed in Great Britain by Clays Ltd, St Ives plc

To Fiona, Jake, Ben and Isaac.

To Fiona, Jake, Ben and Isaac

CHAPTER ONE
EMILY AND LADY GRUBNOT

Emily Cruet knew that dropping a tray of Grubnot's Exclusive crisps could place her in very serious danger. The crisps cascaded down and skittered across the cracked grey lino, their tangy yellow shapes leaping like bouncing bombs. Emily fell to her knees and in desperation started grabbing handfuls of the crisps and putting them back onto the tray, being extremely careful not to break any.

But she'd been seen.

The sound of steel plates on the bottom of pointed shoes started clanking in her direction.

"How DARE you!" shrieked a horribly squawky voice that sounded like a parrot choking on poison. A thumb and forefinger grabbed Emily's left earlobe and, using it as a lever, yanked her to her feet. White-hot pain seared through the viciously squeezed ear.

"It was an accident," said Emily.

The owner of Grubnots Exclusive crisps, Lady Wilhelmina Grubnot, shoved her vulture-like features – ice-blue eyes, thin lips and a short sharp nose that could cut through butter – right into Emily's face. Emily could see every wine line, and could smell her boss's putrid breath. The emerald on the necklace round Lady Grubnot's neck glowed in a ray of light cutting through a production-room window. It seemed to be smirking at Emily's predicament.

"That was no accident!" shrieked Lady Grubnot. "It was a wilful act of sabotage. You intended to strike at the very heart of my magnificent crisp-making enterprise and push production capacity down on delivery day!"

"Lady Grubnot," said Emily's mother, Janet, "she's just a child. Please could you –"

"SILENCE!" roared Lady Grubnot, her hand reaching for the emerald on her neck. Janet gulped and backed away.

"I tripped on the lino," said Emily, unsure whether her ear would remain attached to her head for much longer. "It's got holes in it. It's dangerous."

The veins on Lady Grubnot's neck protruded like a cluster of death-delivering snakes. "No one shall question or criticise any part of my operation, especially a child! I only have to *look* at a child, especially a poor one like you, to be filled with utter REVULSION! No breeding, no manners, plucked from the sewers like a revolting rat, just a charity-seeking leech that steals from me! You did it on purpose – admit it!"

Emily opened her mouth once again to challenge the fiery ear-grabber, but her father, Monty, shook his head vigorously at her. His pleading eyes seemed to leave his face, so keen was he for his daughter to refrain from any further confrontation with the Lady.

"Drop any more of my first-class produce and you will pay, you filthy little being!" snapped Lady Grubnot. "Do you understand me?"

The pupils in Monty's eyes grew larger.

Emily scowled defiantly at Lady Grubnot, but forced herself to mumble, "Yes."

"What was that?"

"I said yes," repeated Emily.

"Well, throw all of the dropped ones away immediately. I can't afford to let any of my customers pick up some disease you've spread onto my crisps by dropping them. A disease-wracked customer could sue me and ruin me. Then make another batch and GET ON WITH IT! Mr Faraday's boat will be here soon."

Lady Grubnot gave Emily's ear another hard squeeze before finally releasing it and storming off to unleash her scythe of a temper on some other unfortunate.

Emily put all of the other spilled crisps onto the tray and emptied the entire batch into a large black dustbin. They dropped into the darkness like a group of explorers toppling over a cliff face and entering a pitch-black forest. What a shocking waste, thought Emily, quickly heading back to join her father at the frying station.

"Are you OK?" asked Paul, the only other child in the room and two years Emily's junior.

"I'm fine," whispered Emily, "let's just get through the rest of the day."

"HURRY UP!" shouted Lady Grubnot, walking among her workers with disdain.

3

Monty gave his daughter a sympathetic nod. She shrugged her shoulders.

Another batch of fresh potatoes was brought in from the storehouse and everyone joined in with washing and peeling them.

Emily's insides bubbled with rage. How she despised Lady Grubnot. How she loathed her. The woman was a despicable tyrant. A spindly boned pile of venom and cruelty. Ever since she could remember, Emily had worked under the seething glare of the Lady, day after day, week after miserable week.

But Emily's fury was tempered by the fact that all of the people she cared for most in the world were right here beside her in this crisp-production room on Grubnot Island: her parents, Janet and Monty; her grandfather, Bob Cruet; her parents' best friends, Simon and Mel Walters; and their son Paul.

Including Emily, that made seven people; seven people who lived and worked together; who wore regulation dark brown trousers, brown coloured shirts, brown boots and brown trilby hats to work; seven people who toiled from 7 a.m. to 6 p.m. in this crisp-production room every single day of the week except Sunday.

These seven people, however, were not just connected because they were family and friends, nor because they all worked together under the hate-soaked eyes of Lady Wilhelmina Grubnot. No, the most powerful thing that tied them together, the thing that fundamentally linked their lives on this secluded island, was the fact that they could never leave.

4

CHAPTER TWO
PAY TIME AND CLEMENCE

As the clock hit six, the last of the week's crisp boxes were stacked on the blades of the orange forklift truck waiting in the loading bay beside the production room. In half an hour or so the forklift would be driven down to the island's south jetty and the boxes would be loaded onto Mr Faraday's boat. He was responsible for getting the Grubnot's Exclusives to the mainland, the start of their journey to the four corners of the planet.

Emily switched off the fryer, where she and her dad spent their days turning ultra-thin raw potato slices into mouth-watering deep-fried snacks. Exhaustion pummelled her bones like an adrenaline-fuelled boxer.

"Right, you ungrateful lot," snapped Lady Grubnot. "Queue up with your greedy hands."

As the workers formed a line, the production-room door opened. In walked a tall, lanky man with grey side-whiskers and thick black glasses. His thin lips were moving in all directions as if he were having a complex discussion with several versions of himself. He was carrying a wicker basket in his left hand and some kind of strange contraption in his right.

This was Clemence.

In most estates the size of Grubnot Island, anything up to thirty members of staff might be employed, but Lady Grubnot liked to keep things simple…and cheap. So Clemence was her only servant. This meant he was her gardener, chef, butler, production-room technician, caretaker, housemaid, window cleaner and entertainment officer, among many other roles. To make Lady Grubnot feel as though she had a large and varied staff she insisted that Clemence wore a different outfit for each task he performed. Thus when she'd summoned him on her ancient walkie-talkie some minutes previously, he'd been wearing a maid's outfit and bonnet as he'd been polishing the silver in the manor-house dining room. When she'd demanded he come to the crisp-production room, he'd hastily changed into his production-room-technician blue overalls and flat grey cap. If a job needed doing on the island, Clemence would do it as soon as he'd got changed into the appropriate outfit.

"Lady Grubnot!" declared Clemence, putting the wicker basket down on a low wooden table. "I am proud to present to you my new, soon-to-be-patented, pay distribution unit." He held up the contraption. It was a small rectangle of steel with a long moveable wooden arm on one side and a mesh of red and green wires on the bottom.

"How many times have I told you?" snarled Lady Grubnot. "I am NOT INTERESTED in your pathetic inventions! I am in the business of making vast sums of money in the quickest time possible!"

"But this will SAVE you time," insisted Clemence, pressing a black button on the side of his contraption. The long wooden arm shot out, slapping Lady Grubnot on the right side of her face with a resounding *thwack*.

She screamed and felt her cheek, which was already starting to go a purplish blue.

"Oh dear!" gasped Clemence, quickly pulling the wooden arm back and examining the wires underneath the box. "The pulleys must have slipped."

"YOU IDIOT!" screamed Lady Grubnot, snatching the machine from Clemence's hands and throwing it at his face. He ducked and the box crashed through a window, sending shards of glass cascading inside and outside the production room.

"CLEAR UP THIS MESS INSTANTLY, YOU IMBECILE!" yelled Lady Grubnot, her entire body shaking with incandescent rage.

Although humour rarely played a part in Emily's working life, at this juncture she couldn't help smiling briefly. Clemence was an odd fellow but unlike Lady Grubnot he seemed to have a heart and his constantly failing inventions were funny to watch, even if he didn't intend them to be. Emily was a bit of an inventor herself, so she'd often thought that she and Clemence might have a lot in common, if only Lady Grubnot allowed her workers to converse with him. But no, this was forbidden, and the only times Emily had spoken to him were five-second snatches of greeting or a brief comment about the weather, when Lady Grubnot was well out of earshot.

"But I don't have my caretaker's outfit on," protested Clemence, "and sweeping up glass falls under janitorial duties rather than crisp-production technician or pay assistant, so maybe I should –"

"JUST DO IT!" shrieked Lady Grubnot, her entire face puce, her fists balled up tightly like coiled hammers of wrath.

Clemence sighed, located a dustpan and brush in a small cupboard near the door and began sweeping up the fragments of glass. While he carried out this duty, Lady Grubnot stood behind the table on which the wicker basket had been placed, and shouted, "PAY TIME!"

The workers had lined up in age order, with Emily's grandfather, Bob, a sprightly seventy-one year old with a fine head of silver hair, at the front. Lady Grubnot reached into the wicker basket and pulled out a mouldy potato with green shoots protruding through its surface. This she handed to Bob, who moved away from the table and walked over to the door. Next up was Janet, Emily's mum, who at forty-seven was the second oldest. Lady Grubnot issued her with a small muddy onion with peeling skin. Monty Cruet, Emily's father, was third in line. Lady Grubnot presented him with a thin and withered carrot. Simon Walters was given a squashed and bruised lemon, while Mel received a rock-hard radish. When Emily, second last – her ear still smarting – put out her hand, she was given a soggy courgette with mottled skin. She frowned but resisted making any comment, clasped it to her chest and went to join the others by the door, turning her head briefly to see Paul getting a shrunken tomato.

Each worker had just been presented with a vegetable that would be rejected by 99.9 per cent of farmers, and one hundred per cent of shoppers, even at the most organic and earth-friendly establishment. These should have been for the trash or the food-recycling bin but each worker held their pay as if it were a precious gem.

And although almost impossible to believe, these pitiful vegetables represented each worker's *entire pay* for that day. That was it: no cash, no food vouchers, no shares in the Grubnot's Exclusive Crisp-Production Company. Nothing.

"Well, what are you waiting for?" snarled Lady Grubnot, eyeing her workers with contempt. "You've been handsomely rewarded for your shoddy work. Now get out of here!"

Emily and the other six stepped outside. Several rays of early evening sunshine were touching the ground and Emily basked in their warmth. At last, a chance to get away from the heat and the bubbling oil, the strict schedules and the marauding menace of the Lady. The air was so much fresher out here. The smell of freshly cut grass and sea air entered her nostrils, and were welcomed with deep appreciation.

This was Emily's favourite time of the week. Not only did she and her co-workers have the whole evening to themselves, tomorrow, Sunday, was their day off – a glorious time when they didn't have to see or hear Lady Grubnot's words or aggressive behaviours, a time during which they wouldn't have to produce a single crisp. It made Emily feel light and liberated – this was her weekly window of freedom and relaxation, the time she craved for almost every second that she spent at work.

While Emily and her fellow workers headed down a cracked gravel path at a leisurely pace, Lady Grubnot hurried in the opposite direction, up a worn, curving track that led to the huge white stuccoed manor house.

"After you've delivered the boxes to the jetty, I want eggs Benedict for supper, Clemence," she snapped at her unfortunate servant. "And this time make sure they're timed to perfection. Last time you burnt them!"

"As you wish," said Clemence, hurrying behind her and desperately trying to remember where he'd left his chef's apron and raised white hat.

CHAPTER THREE
THE YOUNG MISS CRUET YEARS

"How badly does your ear hurt?" asked Janet as she and Emily fell into step together.

"It's not too bad," lied Emily, touching it tenderly and quickly letting it go. It ached like crazy, a pulsing punch of pain.

"I know how much you detest Lady Grubnot, we all do, but answering her back will only make things worse."

Janet smiled weakly and stepped past a pothole on the path.

"Things can't get worse," said Emily, "and I have to say *something* when she accuses me of doing something I didn't do. It *was* an accident when I dropped the tray, Mum. You know I'd never do that on purpose. That floor is a living death trap. Remember when Paul twisted his ankle and had to rest it up for the whole of Sunday and was still hobbling by the Wednesday?"

"Of course I do, but when Lady Grubnot goes into one of her rants, it's not worth challenging her. You know how unpleasant her anger can make her.

Just let it wash over you. It's the only way to deal with her."

"But I can't keep it inside me," said Emily. "It's like a bluebottle trying to get out of a vase. It jumps around inside and has to come out."

Janet put an arm round her daughter's shoulders. "You're young," she said, "and your emotions are all over the place, I understand that. But it's no good. Facing up to her always ends in disaster. We've learnt that through very bitter experience."

"Come on, Mum. Don't be so accepting of it all. Why do you and the other adults just take her insults and screaming fits? Why am I the only one who ever stands up to her?"

"It's just too dangerous," replied Janet, a flicker of fear in her eyes.

"How is it dangerous? And don't tell me it's too complicated to explain." How many times had Emily heard that response?

"It *is* very complicated," sighed Janet, "and there's nothing we can do about it. I wish there was, I really do. But we're in this situation and we need to keep our heads down at work and enjoy the free time we have, just like we've always told you. Verbal jousting with her could be deadly."

Emily groaned. Every time she said anything to challenge Lady Grubnot, this was what she got from her parents and the other adults. Don't rock the boat. It's a deadly game. You'll be putting us all in grave danger. *What are they talking about? Lady Grubnot is an old lady. Why don't we just overpower her, jump onto Mr Faraday's boat and sail away from the island, never to return? Why will no one explain to me what it is they're so afraid of?*

"I saw some chaffinches near the north jetty yesterday," said Paul, catching up with Emily and Janet, unaware of the simmering tension between them. "I think they were a family. They caught these worms and they were sharing them out. Do you want to come with me and see if we can spot them before supper?"

"Thanks but no," said Emily, sullenly kicking a stone into the grass at the side of the path. "I'm really tired. I just want to relax."

For a few seconds Paul looked like a wounded puppy, all drooping face and mournful eyes, but he brightened up quickly. "Maybe tomorrow?"

Emily nodded. "Yes, maybe tomorrow."

As they walked on, Emily suddenly felt smothered by a shroud of loneliness. It wasn't just that she was the only one to take on Lady Grubnot, she also needed a friend. Paul was fine. They'd grown up on this wretched island together. It was the only home they'd ever known. But Paul was younger and Emily had begun to feel the age difference. At times when they talked nowadays, he sounded like someone from a different generation. Over the years they'd spent thousands of hours discussing what life away from the island might be like. There had to be life somewhere other than the island because Mr Faraday and his boat came from somewhere and went back to somewhere. The adults refused to discuss the outside world at all, but even for Emily that conversation had now gone stale; just like everything else on the island. She yearned for an injection of something fresh in her life.

They also had vastly different interests. Emily liked designing and making things from whatever she could find on the island and studying the majestic patterns of stars in the night sky. Her granddad, Bob, had told her all about these and they'd passed many an evening sitting outside with a blanket wrapped around their shoulders, pointing up at the intricate glinting patterns that looked like ancient paintings placed up there for posterity.

Paul liked bird–watching and collecting stones, but these held no interest whatsoever for Emily. In recent weeks she'd begun to feel a powerful need to have someone else to talk to; someone on her wavelength. But being totally isolated on Grubnot Island, with no visitors ever, made this seem as likely as her sprouting wings and learning to fly.

The light was slowly beginning to fade when Emily and the others reached two forks on the path and took the right-hand one. This led them down to a low rectangular wooden shack. A shrill babble of some birds and the faint rustle of an evening breeze accompanied them on this last stage of their journey. With anger, frustration and loneliness prodding her repeatedly, Emily wiped her shoes on the twig mat and stepped inside.

CHAPTER FOUR
THE SHACK

The first thing you noticed when you entered the one-roomed shack was its size. It was very small. Nowhere near big enough for seven people to live comfortably. But these seven weren't your average group of people. Like animals adjusting to a new climate or emerging from a solitary period of hibernation, they had made the best of a bad situation. Four wooden beds stood along one of the longer walls and three along the other, each with a thin mattress, a thin blanket covering a thin sheet, and a thin pillow. It could get seriously cold at night, so Emily had used some large, strong leaves and thin sheets of bark to make hot-water bottles for everyone.

At the far end of the shack was a small kitchenette, with a sink, a narrow work surface, a shelf and a tiny wood-burning cooker with a hob and a small oven. Beyond the kitchenette and behind a white door was a shower. The water only trickled out of this and at best was lukewarm, but it did the job. Beyond the shower was a door that led to an outside toilet.

As the seven workers trooped inside, everyone placed their day's "pay" on the kitchenette's work surface. As it was now dark outside and there was no electricity in the shack, Emily lit six small half-burnt candles that she and Paul had pilfered from the manor-house kitchen and placed these at different points around the shack. She then went into the shower and changed out of her work clothes, garments she detested almost as much as she despised Lady Grubnot. She came back into the room wearing a pair of patched-up jeans and a white T-shirt, shoved her work clothes under her bed and lay down on her mattress.

"I'm on supper duty tonight," announced Monty from the kitchenette, "and it's going to be amazing. The best thing anyone's ever tasted!"

Janet laughed and nudged him in the ribs. "That's what you always say," she chided, "but I don't think Emily will share that opinion. And anyway, it will only taste good because of my efforts with those herbs outside. Let's see what you come up with."

"But I'm the finest chef on this island," grinned Monty, "with or without your herbs. I should win awards and be feted by everyone."

Emily watched this scene and marvelled as always at the way everyone's behaviour and demeanour changed so radically after the working day had finished. It was as if one set of people toiled in the production room and a quite different set lived in this shack. Normally she'd have called out to her father that his prowess as a chef was nothing compared to hers, but she wasn't in the mood for cheery banter. So she stroked her ear and picked up *Pirate Summers and the Coast of Gold*.

The six Pirate Summers books were the only ones Emily had found on the entire island and it was these that her parents had used to teach her to read and write. She never got bored of them because Pirate Summers was such a tough and witty seafarer, the action was swashbuckling, and his archenemy, Captain Half-Eye, was gruesome and deadly. The books mentioned islands and castles and palaces, but nowhere real, and they were the only points of reference Emily had as to what might exist in the rest of the world. Emily had arrived on the island when she was very young. She knew this, as Granddad Bob had once let this slip. But neither he nor any of the other grown-ups would ever talk about what they did before they got here.

Lady Grubnot didn't read books and she shredded newspapers and magazines the minute she'd finished with them. She'd once caught Clemence reading an inventing journal and had set it on fire while it was still in his hands.

Lying on her mattress, Emily managed to lose herself in Pirate Summers's rooftop battle with Captain Half-Eye and before she knew it a delicious smell was wafting through the air. Reading about Pirate Summers's bravery and cunning manoeuvres had taken the edge off her bad temper so she got up and went to investigate. She passed Paul who was sitting on his bed studying a light-grey rock, and Mel who was darning some green socks that had miraculously maintained their colour over the years.

"Smells good!" she said, dipping a finger into the steaming bowl of hot vegetable soup perching on the stove.

"Leave it alone!" grinned Monty, batting her hand away. "You're on supper duty tomorrow and I bet you can't make anything as good as this."

"My meal will be five times tastier," said Emily, "and it'll last twice as long! You have to accept my ingredient-stretching skills are far superior to yours!"

"I accept nothing!" laughed Monty, squeezing her shoulder and looking at her red ear.

"It's OK," Emily said, seeing the concern on his kind and weather-beaten face. "Really."

"Let's get the table set up," said Janet.

"I hate her for doing that to you," sighed Monty.

"It's not the end of the world," said Emily.

The expression on her father's narrow face seemed to suggest that if it wasn't quite as bad as that, remaining motionless while your daughter was ferociously attacked was pretty near the end of the world.

Emily moved to a large wooden structure leaning against the wall and wheeled it into the small space that stood between the kitchen area and the first beds.

"I'll do my end first," said Emily, carefully unfolding a section of the wood. Janet came to join her and mirrored her move with the opposite section. Within moments a round table stood in front of them – a structure they were rather pleased with, as it was they who'd created it. They then grabbed seven chairs that they'd made from the same batch of wood. Clemence in lumberjack mode had been instructed to chop down several trees two summers ago. The lumberjack trousers and boots he'd worn were very comfortable, but the blue and green checked shirt had been annoyingly itchy.

With the table and chairs set up, everyone began migrating to the source of the inviting aroma. As they took their places, Monty ladled out his soup into bark bowls and handed round small rolls he'd made with the last batch of yeast filched from the manor house.

Emily spooned up a tiny morsel of soup and placed it directly on top of her taste buds. The flavour zinged along her tongue, lighting up her mouth and sending sparks of warmth and content-edness to the furthest nerve endings of her body. It was a magnificent sensation and it took a while for her to allow the delicious liquid to slide down her throat and make its way to her belly, which was beating a drum for sustenance.

A full globe of a silver, pockmarked moon outside provided strips of light to complement the candles, and everyone's face was bathed in warmth and shadow.

"It's not too bad," commented Emily, adding a tiny dash of salt to her portion, "but I'd have seasoned it slightly differently, Dad."

"You're on supper tomorrow," hit back Monty, "and I'm looking forward to seeing what you come up with, different seasoning or not."

"You two are crazy," grinned Simon Walters, breaking his bread roll in two. "Maybe this competition is just a father and daughter thing."

"I think it's healthy," chipped in Bob. "Youngsters should always keep adults on their toes, don't you think, Emily?"

"Absolutely." said Emily. "Especially when they're better cooks!"

"Now, now," said Janet, "that's enough for one meal."

"Fair enough," said Emily. "But you know I'm better."

"I think I am," laughed Monty.

Emily realised she was now in a far, far lighter mood than the one she'd been in after the mini-clash with her mum; food often had a way of eradicating grouchiness. But the questions about Lady Grubnot and what kind of dangers her workers faced on the island were still swooping and circling in her mind.

As she took another mouthful, she felt that if she didn't get some answers pretty soon she might just well explode. And if that happened, she probably wouldn't be able to cook supper tomorrow night.

CHAPTER FIVE
A DISCOVERY

"Let's get those crisps frying," said Monty.

Emily flicked a red dial on the side of the big metal fryer and the oil inside soon started bubbling. She studied the needle on a panel on the front. The oil needed to heat to exactly 180 degrees centigrade. Not 179.9 or 180.01 but 180 exactly. This was Lady Grubnot's rule and it was non-negotiable.

"OK, Dad." She nodded when the needle hit 180. "Over to you."

Monty lowered a metal tray, on which sat hundreds of wafer-thin potato slices, into the boiling oil and another batch of crisps was on the go.

The weekend was over and it was Monday morning. The first day of another week of dreaded working. Emily rolled up her sleeves and made sure the temperature stayed constant. All around her was the sound and movement of earnest industry. Staged in isolation, their individual activities were worthless. Melded together, and they became the recipe for some of the world's most incredibly flavoursome snacks.

The production room was the size of a medium-sized school hall, rectangular in shape, its walls lined with peeling white paint. There were windows round its perimeter but these were grimy and caked with dust. As a result they let in very little natural light, so old-fashioned ceiling strip lights illuminated the space with a pale-yellow glow. It had the feel of a shabby wartime industrial unit, halted by time and in urgent need of repair.

The production process worked as follows. All seven workers brought the potatoes in from the storeroom and washed them under leaky taps attached to cracking grey pipes. The workers then separated and took up positions at their own sta-tions. Janet gouged out any stones and impurities. Bob peeled the spuds. Simon sliced them into strips exactly 1.2 millimetres thick. Mel washed away any excess starch. Paul dried them, then placed them on a steel trolley and pushed this over to Emily and Monty, the fryers.

All of the machinery used to make these crisps might as well have come from a time capsule left by a stone-age community; it was blunt, rusty and misshapen, not to mention exceedingly dangerous. Lady Grubnot refused to pay a penny for its upkeep or repair so it was up to her workers to service their instruments and take great care to avoid injury. Many a time Emily and her father had narrowly escaped severe burns when tempestuous droplets of oil sprang out of the fryer, searching for some-one to brandish. Minor burns they could just about tolerate.

When the frying was complete, Emily and Monty wheeled a trolley with the finished items over to a white line. Lady Grubnot then unlocked the door to a high security room called the seasoning cupboard, taking the crisps inside and locking the door firmly. It was in here that she added the seasonings she had conjured up in the mixing tower, a tall cylindrical building some distance behind the production room, which stood on a grass mound surrounded by razor wire.

But while Emily hated Lady Grubnot and the crisp-production room as much as her fellow workers did, there was an extra factor that affected her alone. Whereas the others had been put off crisps many years ago, Emily absolutely *adored* them. This should have been something of a joy as the young girl was surrounded by vast helpings of the sliced potato snacks. But Emily's yearning was never fulfilled because the truth was she'd only ever tasted *one* crisp in her entire life. That had been four years ago and she remembered the moment with absolute clarity.

It had been a Saturday morning and she'd found herself in a quiet corner of the production room. After avoiding the temptation to eat one for so long and convinced that no one could see her, she popped a wild-mushroom-flavoured crisp into her mouth. Within seconds it was as if a box of fireworks had just been ignited on her tongue. The crisp tasted sensational, yes of mushrooms, but also of country pastures, open fires and silvery salt. It instantly made Emily want to eat more, many, many more, and she was about to scoop up an entire handful when she discovered that Lady Grubnot had been spying on her workers from a secret perch near the ceiling of the production room. After screaming at Emily from on high like a crazed preacher of doom, Lady Grubnot had raced downstairs and declared that, as a result of Emily's wanton thievery, she would work an extra eleven-hour shift, by herself, on a Sunday. Emily's parents had interceded, pleading with Lady Grubnot to allow one of them to take the shift instead of their daughter, but the Lady had touched the emerald round her neck and Monty and Janet had stepped back, looks of horror plastered over their faces.

Since then Emily had never tasted another crisp. This was at times unbearable as she could smell their scintillating flavours and see their inviting golden shapes wherever she looked. In her favourite day-dream she dived head first into a gigantic mound of the flavorous snacks and devoured as many as she could. But she knew that this vision was no more than a bitter 1.2-millimetre slice of wishful thinking that would never come true. Her grave would probably be made of potato peelings and bear a sign stating: SHE FRIED.

The end of that Monday came as a mighty relief to Emily but her mother stopped her as they walked down the path after work.

"Where are you going?" asked Janet, as everyone made for the right fork while Emily headed for the left.

"I want to get some air," said Emily, her brow knitted as if someone had painted a long line on her forehead.

"You can sit round the back of the shack with me, that's fresh air."

"I want to be alone for a while. No offence. I just need a bit of space."

"Fine." Janet said. "But make sure you're back in time for supper and don't stray from the paths."

There it was again. It was maddening. Don't touch the fence surrounding the island. Don't go anywhere near the emerald around her neck. A constant onslaught of warnings.

Hurrying away from the others, for a second she was tempted to leap through the air and land in the forbidden grass beyond the paths, just to see what happened. But the fear in the warnings the adults issued held her back. Maybe not knowing was a preferable option.

She decided to head to the eastern edge of the estate. She hadn't been there for a while. It took her ten minutes to follow several tarmac tracks, past unkempt hedgerows and large patches of withering blue flowers. When she reached the end of the main eastern path, she found herself staring up at a clump of gnarled oak trees that looked like a group of ancient sages, huddled together, muttering darkly among themselves. Just beyond the trees was a dense collection of gorse bushes and she was about to sit down on the path for a rest when she spotted a flash of grey.

Frowning, she stepped forward, knelt down and pulled the first two bushes aside. To her surprise, parting the green waves uncovered a completely overgrown path – a path she had never seen before.

She hesitated for a second. Because this path was hidden from view, did it still count as a "safe" path or was it in some way dangerous? And why had it been allowed to vanish underneath this great green canopy? She let go of the bushes, stood up and pursed her lips. Was this a sinister trap set by Lady Grubnot? If Emily stepped onto this newly discovered path would she get hurt – or worse? She scratched her cheek uncertainly but her sense of adventure eventually nudged her anxiety aside.

Looking round to make sure there was no one else in the vicinity, she listened for human sounds. All she heard was a murmur from some rustling grass and a bird chirruping some way away. Everything else was perfectly still. Reaching out, she pushed aside the first two bushes again. They were waist high. With trembling legs she took her first steps on the covered-up path. Her heart jolted with a mix of fear and excitement. The chance to do something new, anything new, was intoxicating! The path felt solid beneath her feet so she separated the next bushes and moved slowly forward, stealing a glance over her shoulder every now and then to make sure she was still alone. The path curved to the right, to the left and then straightened up. It was at this point that it became clear to Emily where it ended: right next to the fence, a huge wooden structure topped with vicious razor wire.

Don't stray from the paths. Don't touch the fence.

OK, thought Emily, *I won't touch the fence, but I can go right up to it, can't I? No one's ever said don't*

26

do that. Bush after bush she swept aside, ignoring the tough stems and harsh leaves that jabbed at her knees.

A few minutes later she was less than two metres from the fence. She looked back and saw that all of the bushes had closed again, like a line of dancers who had just pirouetted back into their starting positions. The path was now completely invisible to anyone who might arrive at the scene. And if someone did show up all she would need to do was kneel down on this hidden path to erase herself from view.

She was just getting used to being in such close proximity to the dreaded fence when a voice suddenly demanded, "Is that your school uniform?"

CHAPTER SIX

ZAK

Emily was so taken aback that she spun round in panic, convinced the voice belonged to Lady Grubnot. Had she crept up on Emily and was about to pounce? Was she going to issue some draconian punishment? *But hang on a second,* thought Emily, *the voice didn't come from behind me, it came from the* other side of the fence. *And it didn't sound at all like Lady Grubnot's. Nor Clemence's for that matter.* But if it wasn't Lady Grubnot or Clemence, then who exactly was it? After all, apart from those two, Mr Faraday (on a couple of occasions), the postman once and her six co-workers, Emily had never come across anyone else.

"If it *is* your school uniform it looks weird," continued the boy's voice, for it was definitely a boy. "In fact, the last time anyone wore a hat like that to school was probably a hundred years ago! Is it some kind of private prep school or something?"

Emily followed the voice's trajectory and spied a small hole in the fence a metre off the ground. Filling the hole was a single eye. Emily hesitated for a few seconds, fear lapping at her insides.

But then, kneeling down a little way back from the fence, she took a closer look at the eye. It was hazel green with two tiny flecks of brown above the pupil. The pupil moved as it looked Emily up and down.

"You're not *touching* the fence are you?" she asked.

"No way," replied the voice. "Mr Faraday says it's deadly dangerous; he reminds me about it every week. To tell you the truth, it gets a bit on my nerves the way he goes on about it."

Emily was staggered by the fact that she was actually having a conversation with a stranger, someone from the "Outside".

"I know what you mean," said Emily. "I get warned off the fence on a daily basis. Do you work for Lady Grubnot?" Suspicion framed her words. Who was this boy, and would talking to him result in her getting into heaps of trouble?

"Sort of," replied the boy, his eye blinking several times. "I help Mr Faraday with the pick-ups of those crisp boxes, and the deliveries of food and stuff to Lady Grubnot and that funny chap who works for her, Clemence. We come this time from Northurst Bay every Saturday."

Emily had heard Lady Grubnot and Clemence talking about Northurst. It was the nearest piece of land to the island. But when they mentioned it, it felt as if it was some kind of imagined place. Now the boy had spoken of it, it suddenly felt very real.

"I didn't know anyone else lived on the island," he added.

"Does Mr Faraday know you're here?" asked Emily.

"He's tinkering with his boat right now so I thought I'd go for a stroll. Ever since I've worked for him I've wanted to know what's on the other side of this fence. About a minute ago I spotted this hole and then I heard footsteps on the other side so I had to take a look. That's when I saw you and your funny brown uniform. Your school must be stuck in the Victorian age or something."

Emily gulped. *Can I trust this boy? Might he be a stooge of Lady Grubnot's?* She chewed her bottom lip uncertainly and then hesitantly said, "What's your name?"

"It might be Zak," he replied, "but then again, it might not."

"I'm Emily."

"So *is* that your school uniform?" asked Zak (or maybe not Zak).

"Sorry," said Emily, "I don't know that word you're using."

"Which word?"

"School."

"Excuse me?"

"School," repeated Emily, "what does it mean?" Emily had never heard her parents, or anyone else for that matter, using it.

"Are you making fun of me?" snapped Zak.

His eye suddenly disappeared from the hole.

"NO! WAIT, DON'T GO!" pleaded Emily, placing her eye as near to the hole as she dared. The figure she saw standing on the other side was a slim boy about her height with a great curtain of blond hair swept across his forehead, and turquoise eyes that were narrowed

30

with mistrust. He was dressed in faded jeans, a big white T-shirt bearing a picture of a menacing-looking green animal, black trainers and an orange peaked cap. He stood on a sloping grassy bank that led down to the edge of a vast expanse of water. It was the first time Emily had ever seen the water, as the workers on Grubnot Island were forbidden from going anywhere near the gates when Mr Faraday's boat was there or at any other time. The blue seemed to go on forever; there were no boats, no inlets, no islands in sight. How she would have loved to climb over the fence, run down to the water's edge and wash her face in the coolness of that tantalising ocean.

"I'm not making fun of you," Emily insisted. "I've just never heard it before."

There was silence for a few seconds.

"Promise you're not trying to wind me up," said Zak, taking a deep breath and huffing it out. "Some of the kids at school do that just because I'm a bit slower at reading and writing than them." He turned the toe of his right trainer in the grass.

"I promise," said Emily.

"So if you really don't know the word 'school', does that mean you don't *go* to one?"

"If I don't know what one is I can't very well go to one, can I?" pointed out Emily, not unreasonably.

"You are SO lucky," said Zak, shaking his head in wonder, still not sure whether to believe this strangely dressed girl or not.

"So, what *is* school?" enquired Emily.

"It's a place where kids go and grown-ups teach them stuff. You know, how to read and write and

31

do sums and things. A lot of the time it's boring, but playtime's OK. You have to go there every day, Monday to Friday, from nine a.m. to three-thirty p.m."

"So when do you do your job?" asked Emily.

"Is this some sort of wind-up?" shot back Zak, his hackles rising again.

"No, I just want to know about your work."

"Kids don't work out here. You must know that. I mean, they do Saturday jobs, like me with Mr Faraday, but that's about it."

"I work from seven a.m. to six p.m. from Monday to Saturday in Lady Grubnot's crisp-production room," said Emily.

"Seriously?"

"Absolutely."

"How much does she pay you?"

"One mouldy vegetable per day."

"I knew you were making fun of me!" snarled Zak, his top lip curling in anger.

"It's the truth!" insisted Emily. "That's all we get. Today I was paid a squashed off-red tomato."

Zak frowned and Emily heard him say the words "squashed off-red tomato" under his breath.

Just then came the rumble of the forklift trundling its way down to the south jetty. Clemence would be at the wheel, on a mission to deliver a huge stack of crisp boxes to the waiting boat.

"If you're telling me the truth, that doesn't sound right at all," he finally declared. "A kid working incredibly long hours for pay as pathetic as that sounds very, very wrong. I'm going to tell Mr Faraday about it and get him to call the authorities when we get back to the mainland."

"You can't do that!" cried Emily, who didn't know what the authorities were but didn't like the sound of them. "It would put us all in great danger."

"Why?"

"I'm not sure, but my parents say Lady Grubnot has the power to destroy us all if we ever get a chance to tell anyone. I've probably already said far too much."

"The woman sounds like a complete menace," snarled Zak. "She's out of her mind."

"Promise me you won't tell anyone," said Emily.

"OK." Zak nodded. "I won't tell anyone. But I don't like it at all. It stinks."

At that instant a horn started beeping impatiently.

Zak gulped, spun round and started sprinting away.

"HEY!" called Emily. "WHERE ARE YOU GOING?"

"It's Mr Faraday!" he shouted. "I've got to go!"

"Well...well...can we meet up again?" cried Emily, her voice laced with panic. Now that she'd spoken to this boy, the thought of never speaking to him again was pure agony. It was like opening a jar of honey and having it snatched away from you by a marauding bear. She couldn't let this conversation be a one-time occurrence. "Same time next Saturday?"

Zak shouted something back, but the wind carried his words out of earshot and a moment later he'd hared round the curve and gone from view.

Emily stayed where she was without moving a muscle, joint or tendon, keenly aware that what had just happened was possibly the most exciting event in her life so far. It was bigger than big and both crucially vital and vitally crucial. She stood there, trying to take in the conversation. Five of Zak's words were pounding through her brain.

Kids don't work out here.

Was that true? If it was, it was almost beyond comprehension. And what about that school place? It sounded amazing. Fancy being able to spend your days learning stuff instead of frying potato slices! Emily felt as if a parachute had suddenly wrapped up her brain and body and dropped them into a new and unexplored world. Imagine not working.

A short while later she heard the revving of an engine and somewhere out of sight Mr Faraday's boat started speeding back to Northurst Bay with Zak on board. Realising it was getting dark, Emily remembered she'd told her mum she'd be back by supper time. Quickly she made her way back through the gorse bushes and stepped off the over-grown path, throwing some leaves over its entrance so it was as hidden as before.

It was almost totally dark by the time she got back to the shack, snippets from her conversation with Zak flitting through her mind like pulses of colour and light. For years she'd wanted to meet someone from the outside world and now she had. She really had. But the question was: would she ever see him again?

CHAPTER SEVEN
BOXING UP THE PAST

"**A** re you OK?" asked Bob.

It was later that night and Emily was in her pyjamas, sitting cross-legged on her bed, staring into space, mesmerised by the encounter she'd experienced just a couple of hours ago. She'd had a conversation with someone new. OK, it was conducted through a hole in the fence but, unless she'd dreamed it, it really had taken place. She felt like Pirate Summers must have felt when he finally got his hands on the Ruby Sword of Life after years spent trying to track down its secret location. And Zak's mention of "school" and the disgusted way he talked about Lady Grubnot had set off sparks within her. He came from elsewhere; from somewhere that wasn't Grubnot Island; from another world. He'd told her there was another way of living where you didn't have to fry crisps endlessly and get stung by flying drips of scalding oil.

Her granddad sat on the bed beside her and gave her a concerned look.

For a minute she was tempted to tell him everything but she knew this wouldn't be a wise course of action. He and the adults were so jumpy about the fence and the paths and everything else that if she did mention her meeting with Zak he'd probably tell the others and they'd try to stop her from seeing him again. There was no way she could allow that to happen. Zak and the hole in the fence had to remain her secret, at least for now.

"I'm fine, just tired," replied Emily.

"Fancy a game of chess?" asked Bob. "I can't believe I only taught you last summer on that set you made, and now you're beating me."

"I will play you, but not tonight."

"Fair enough. I'll need to sharpen my game before we meet again. I now know all about your favourite opening and that last row checkmate trick."

On the bed next to hers, Mel Walters clacked her knitting needles together as she was making a new sweater for Paul. The clink of plates came from the kitchenette where Janet was doing the washing up.

"I'm not better than you," smiled Emily. "I just try to talk to you when you're planning your next move. It's a sneaky way to unfocus you!"

"I can't believe you do that, you crafty girl! That's nigh on cheating. You little rapscallion!"

Bob looked at the stack of Pirate Summers books on the floor by her bed. "I'm sorry we haven't ever managed to get you anything else to read," he sighed. "When I was a boy I had loads of books."

"Tell me what it was like when you were a boy, Granddad?" pleaded Emily.

"Don't worry about that," said Bob, blushing, as if mentioning his own childhood would unleash an ancient curse, the sort that appeared in *Pirate Summers and the Ghostly Force*.

"It doesn't have to be a full family history," groaned Emily, "just a few stories about where you grew up and what it was like."

"How are you doing with the outdoor table you're making?" asked Bob, quickly changing the subject.

"I'll tell you about it another time," she replied.

She climbed into bed, pulled the covers over her and lay on her side, facing away from him. Two could play at this game of silence and evasion.

"You're a great kid," he said, ruffling the hair on the back of her head, "but some things are better left alone."

She didn't reply.

On Tuesday, Lady Grubnot shouted at Emily for being slow and Emily told her she was working as fast as she could. On Wednesday, Lady Grubnot criticised her and Monty's frying technique and Emily hit back that they were experts at their job. She got pinched on the underside of her arm for this retort. When the Lady tugged Paul's hair for not moving fast enough, Monty had to hold Emily back, so great was her rage.

"Please, Emily," said Janet as they sat outside the shack that night. "You've got to stop doing this. Lady

Grubnot is so unpredictable. She's capable of doing anything. Rile her too much and it could all end in disaster for us. Just do your job and steer clear of her. Don't give her any reason to lose her temper."

"She loses it all the time!" snapped Emily. "It doesn't take anything to get her going."

"Please, Emily."

"No! We work in that dangerous factory for hours and hours each week with mouldy vegetables for pay. She treats us like dirt, particularly Paul and me, and I can't stand it any longer. I'll keep answering her back, and I'll get louder and more ferocious in the way I do it unless you tell me the reason we're here, trapped in this awful life of drudgery and fear. I mean it, Mum. I *need* to know. None of you talk about your past lives; none of you say anything about life away from the island. But there must be some kind of life out there. Mr Faraday doesn't take the crisp boxes nowhere. There MUST be another way of living."

An image of Zak appeared in her mind.

Kids don't work out here.

Janet was silent for a few minutes and Emily felt the familiar disappointment slithering into her heart. Was this going to be another blanket of silence, a refusal to answer her questions? Please, no more of this shutting down.

"I'm twelve years old, Mum," she continued, sensing a tiny chink in her mum's defensive armour. "I work the same hours as you. I get the same pay. I'm treated in the same way. I've got a right to know. It would help me so much to know our history. It would answer all of those nagging questions that drive me mad. Go on, Mum. I'm begging you."

Janet said nothing for a while and Emily felt tension crackling in the night air.

"Please, Mum."

"You know what," Janet finally said, placing her hands on the side of her cheeks and gazing at her daughter. "I think you might be right, Emily. You are still a child but you've had to grow up pretty quickly here and, yes, I think on balance you probably do have a right to know."

Emily shivered in the night breeze. Had she pushed her mum far enough? Might this be the moment she'd yearned for? She felt an invisible swirl of tension hovering between her and Janet. Come on. Just tell me!

"The one thing holding me back is that I don't know how you'll feel if I *do* tell you," said Janet. "I'll be taking a big risk. We've kept silent on this subject because we want to protect you. You might not be able to handle the truth." Her mother's eyes were filled with concern. "I don't want to damage you."

Zak told me about school and I didn't freak out, thought Emily. "I can take it, whatever it is, Mum. I'd prefer to know and be upset, than to not know and be even more upset. I reckon any damage to me was done way back."

Her mother's softening expression sent a pulse of excitement dancing through her. "Come on, Mum, tell me!"

"OK," sighed Janet, "I will tell you. I just hope it's a decision I don't come to regret."

"You won't regret it," said Emily, sensing that another of the most important episodes in her life was about to begin. After waiting so long was she about to hear the history. The truth. Her body trembled with excitement.

Janet folded her hands on her lap, composed herself and then closed her eyes. Twenty seconds later she opened them and took a good look at her daughter, hoping with all of her heart that Emily would be able to take on what she was about to tell her.

"OK," she said.

And then she began.

CHAPTER EIGHT
LADY GRUBNOT'S STORY

"Lady Grubnot's father, Lord Fortescue Grubnot, was born here on this island estate, like his father and his grandfather before him," said Janet. "The Grubnots are closely related to the royal family – any living Grubnot is pretty high up in the pecking order of heirs to the throne."

Emily raised her eyebrows. She'd heard Lady Grubnot muttering about the royals before but she'd had no idea the Lady was actually *related* to them.

"Unlike some very wealthy people, Fortescue's parents didn't use nannies or servants to bring him up. They were totally 'hands on.' And in spite of being born into immense privilege they instilled in him the need to help others, particularly children in difficult circumstances. His was an extremely happy childhood. His parents loved him dearly and he loved them back.

"Sadly, they both died in a car crash when he was only nine and he had to grow up very quickly. He had a wonderful governess called Miss Jessop, who showed him all of the love and care his parents had lavished on him and she continued their excellent work in pointing his moral compass in the right direction. Fortescue grew up to be a strong character and he fulsomely adopted his parents' charitable disposition. From the age of sixteen he started contributing time and money to charities that helped disadvantaged children. Several years later he met a generous and sparky young woman called Arabella Palmer in a soup kitchen for homeless teenagers. After a short courtship, they married and had a daughter, whom they named Wilhelmina."

"Lady Wilhelmina Grubnot?" exclaimed Emily. "Her parents were those two lovely charitable people?"

Janet nodded. "Sometimes lovely parents can produce ogres."

"Go on, go on!" pleaded Emily, her eyes locked with almost super-human intensity on her mother's.

"Wilhelmina was a difficult baby and an even harder toddler, moody and whiny and aggressive. But Fortescue and Arabella attended to her every need, while maintaining all of their charitable commitments. They took her to many royal gatherings at various palaces and castles, but they watched in despair as she stole toys from the other royal children, bit them and pushed them, not to mention being rude and demanding to the adults. In spite of their efforts to tame her, Wilhelmina burnt holes in palace carpets, swung from priceless chandeliers and painted crayon pictures over fifteenth-century writing bureaus. Her favourite party trick though was to throw and smash things, like teacups and glasses, against fireplaces, doors and walls, acts she enjoyed so much more if she knew the object to be obliterated was very valuable, either financially or sentimentally, or both."

"She sounds awful," said Emily, "even as a small child."

"When Wilhelmina was six," continued Janet, "Fortescue was visiting a home for orphaned children in Dublin, Ireland, when he came across a noisy and excitable group of people standing outside the Tayto crisp factory. Apparently its owner, Joe 'Spud' Murphy, and one of his workers, Seamus Burke, had invented a method for *flavouring* crisps – something that had never been done before. The crowd was made up of foreign crisp manufacturers, business people who wanted to pay Spud for the right to use his flavouring processes in their own countries.

"As Fortescue stood there an idea suddenly leapt into his head. Lots of the underprivileged children he and Arabella visited *adored* crisps but most of them couldn't afford to buy any. Sure, a packet of crisps wouldn't change anyone's life but it would put a smile on their face. So two hours later, Fortescue – along with several of the business people – left the Tayto factory with less money, but with the secret flavouring techniques and recipes safely stashed in their overcoat pockets. Fortescue had told Spud that he would not be using the formula to make *mass-produced* crisps. It was going to be a very small and totally private enterprise in which money would not change hands. The crisps would be free gifts for the underprivileged. So Fortescue would not be competing in any way with Spud's Tayto produce."

"Hang on," said Emily, "how do you know about all of this stuff. Did Lady Grubnot tell you?"

Janet shook her head. "In our early days here I sometimes helped out at the manor house with the cleaning and I found an old blue notebook wedged down the side of a desk, in which she'd written all of this down. I'm only relating the main points, mind you."

Emily nodded for her mother to continue.

"Returning to Grubnot Island, Fortescue and Arabella set up a small crisp-making operation and started producing flavoured crisps in brightly coloured packets for the children they visited. The delight on the children's faces when they received the crisps was enough to make Fortescue and Arabella think that they had made an excellent decision."

"And that's how the crisp-production room started!" gasped Emily.

Janet nodded. "Their daughter however was not happy. Her behaviour worsened and just after her ninth birthday she broke into her father's study and started rifling through his documents. It wasn't long before she discovered the sums of money her parents were giving away to charity. This incensed her. What were they playing at? The more money they gave away the less money there would be left for her when they died. She confronted them most bitterly about this.

"Her parents listened to her screeching and wailing and carefully explained that she had hundreds of benefits unavailable to these poor children and that they deserved whatever help they could get. And anyway, there would be plenty of money left for her in their wills. Suffice it to say, she did not accept this explanation and her tantrums grew in physical wildness and decibel levels. At the next royal function – this one a prince's birthday tea – Wilhelmina, still seething about the financial discoveries in her parents' study, smashed an entire eleventh-century china set by throwing it at a grand piano, in addition to cutting one of the younger princes' hair with a fork. The royal family, who had tolerated her until then, took great offence at these actions and immediately banned her, but not her parents, from attending any future royal events. This incensed her even more than her parents' charitable endeavours, and by the time she entered her teens she was a foulmouthed, obnoxious young person. Her parents continued to try to get through to her and curtail her mad rages and violent actions, but their efforts were in vain. After years of berating Fortescue and Arabella for their stingy and selfish parenting skills, she entered her twenties, angrier than ever.

"Why did they keep trying to help her when she was so mean to them?" asked Emily, shuffling in her seat and studying the shadow that had fallen across her mother's face. "Why didn't they just give up?"

"They were unusually dedicated people," replied Janet. "They still thought that they might have a small chance of redeeming her."

"So what happened next?"

"Her parents continued to give large sums to charity but kept on detailing the generous financial provisions they'd made for her. But she refused to listen. She was so convinced that they'd leave her penniless, she decided she would have to make some money of her own. But instead of getting a job, as most people would do, she took up gambling. At first she did well but over time she began to lose large amounts of money. When she asked her parents to pay off her gambling debts they refused. These debts got bigger and bigger and reached a point where if she didn't pay them off she would land herself in prison."

"*Did* she go to prison?" asked an enthralled Emily.

Janet shook her head. "Two weeks later her parents both caught a rare virus and died within three days of each other. However, rather than mourning their loss, Wilhelmina, or now *Lady* Wilhelmina – as her father's title was hereditary – rushed back to Grubnot Island in delight. At last she'd be able to pay off her debts with the money her parents had always promised they'd leave her. But Wilhelmina's appalling behaviour over the years had ground her parents down so far that they had left every single penny to the various charities they supported. In addition, they inserted a clause in their will prohibiting her from selling a single millimetre of the estate. In short, they had completely disinherited her and she was left with nothing."

"She must have been crushed," murmured Emily.

"She was overflowing with fury." Janet nodded. "How could they have done this to her? She was massively in debt, she had the threat of the bailiffs and prison hanging over her and here were her mother and father, laughing at her from their freshly dug graves. It was an act of gargantuan outrageousness and despicable financial cruelty. As she stormed round the estate in a fearful rage she finally found herself in the crisp-making room and an idea was born. She could use this place. She could start making crisps herself. But she wouldn't give them out free to filthy, undeserving children; she would make them to generate money, mountains of the stuff. She would become a titan of the crisps industry, a self-made businesswoman who would never need a morsel of financial assistance from anyone ever again. But there was one snag. As she wasn't prepared to do any of the actual crisp-making herself, she would need workers."

"This is where we all come in, isn't it?" said Emily. This was going to be it. THE answer to THE question.

Janet sighed and nodded. "At that time, your dad, granddad and I, and Simon and Mel Walters, were all working at the Foxter car plant in Northurst, across the water. Things seemed to be going well and the management were pleased with our efforts and the factory's productivity. But then quite suddenly Foxter's lost a very large German contract and the firm began to lose money. The managers were decent people – they weren't prepared to ride roughshod over us and they tried desperately to keep the place going. But it was no good; the order book was emptying and the factory was forced to close.

It was a devastating blow to us. You were only eighteen months old and Mel was pregnant with Paul. We had no savings and no relatives who could help us out. How would we pay the rent on our houses? How would we eat? We were in a terrible quandary; and that's when your dad saw the advert in the local paper."

"What advert?"

"It read: 'Needed, small group of workers to set up an exciting new business on Grubnot Island. Excellent rates of pay, full board and lodgings provided,'" recited Janet. "We'd all heard of Grubnot Island and had seen Lord Fortescue and Lady Arabella Grubnot at several official functions in the town, as well as read snippets about them in the newspapers, mainly concerning their charitable work. We all knew they had died but of their daughter, Lady Wilhelmina Grubnot, we knew nothing. No one had ever seen her, let alone spoken to her. Somehow, all of her gambling troubles and bad behaviour had been kept out of the press. The advert your dad spotted appeared to be the lifeline we were seeking. We were a small group of workers in need of work. The excellent rates of pay and full board and lodgings sounded like generous reward for this exciting new business. Your father immediately phoned Lady Grubnot and had a very friendly and positive conversation with her. She sounded kind and genuine and the terms she was offering were even better than we had imagined. She told us to be at bay eighteen, Northurst Harbour, at five-thirty p.m. the following day."

"So you went there?"

"Absolutely. We used our redundancy money from the car factory to pay off the rent we owed, packed whatever we could into a few suitcases and made for the harbour. It was a glorious summer day. The heat was just right, not too hot but warm enough to enjoy, and the water looked like a huge blue sheet of perfectly smooth glass. A gaudily decorated red-and-white boat sailed into view and we watched it moor at bay eighteen, where we were waiting with our suitcases. I was carrying you in my arms and Mel was carrying a large bump in her belly. And there she was: a smiling and most welcoming Lady Grubnot, who helped us carry our suitcases onto her boat."

"But what did Lady Grubnot say about there being an eighteen-month-old child there and a woman who was clearly pregnant?" asked Emily, reeling at the details of this story. "Wasn't she worried that these two things would slow her business down? Couldn't she see that you would have to look after me and that Mel wouldn't be able to work for some time after she had her baby?"

"She hardly glanced at you – she was that desperate to get going. When we landed at the north jetty on Grubnot Island she was still full of good cheer and she opened the massive gates and led us in. But before we knew it, the gates had clanged shut, her welcoming expression had vanished and she told us the terrible truth. We were to work in her crisp-production room for an absolute pittance to enable her to pay off her gambling debts and create a huge fortune for her. She showed us the shack where we would all be living and issued us with uniforms she'd bought in a factory closure sale on the mainland. We were dumbstruck. We couldn't believe it. She'd cheated us terribly. It was like we'd all stepped into a terribly warped nightmare."

"But why didn't you just go back to the jetty and take her boat to the mainland?" demanded Emily. "Or overpower her? There were five of you and only one of her."

Janet sighed. "During the Second World War, Grubnot Island was used as a munitions factory. They made hundreds of bombs here. Lady Grubnot told us that she had planted unexploded bombs all over the grass but away from the main paths, and that the fence was trip-wired with dynamite as well as carrying a lethal, high-voltage electrical current. If we stepped off the paths or tried to scale the fence we'd be blown to smithereens or electrocuted for our troubles. Plus, the emerald pendant she wore round her neck had a switch to detonate everything all at once. If we so much as tried to touch her, contact anyone to tell them the truth, or make an attempt to escape, she would press it and blow us all, including herself, sky high."

"So *that's* why we have to stick to the paths and not touch the fence," said Emily. "And *that's* why you always back off when she touches her emerald."

Janet nodded.

"How did you know she was telling the truth about all those bombs, the tripwires and the electrical circuit? Has anyone ever tested any of it out?"

"In that first week, Simon did place a fingertip against the fence and he got a very bad electrical shock. No one's been near it ever since."

I have, thought Emily. *I've been right next to it!*

"And that's the wretched tale of how we got here," sighed Janet. "Are you pleased I told you or are you very upset?"

Emily thought about this for a few moments. "It's shocking," she said, "but I much prefer knowing than not knowing. It's bugged me all of these years and now it will help me make sense of lots of things: the way we live, the reason she can get away with being so awful to us, the fear."

"Please don't say anything to Paul. It's up to Simon and Mel when they tell him, OK?"

Emily nodded. "Does Dad feel terribly guilty about answering that advert?"

"A day never passes when he doesn't think about it," said Janet, "but it's not his fault. We all agreed that taking up Lady Grubnot's offer was the best way forward at that time. If only we'd known what a sinister character she was."

"She's doubly evil," said Emily. "She trapped us and then she made us work for her. She can't have any feelings at all."

"While you let all of this sink in," added Janet, "it's also probably best not to say anything to Dad and Granddad. Dad feels bad enough about it already without knowing that you now know. It's not a case of lying, it's just about withholding a bit of information."

"Fine. I'm just pleased you told me."

Janet stood up and shivered. "Come on, it's pretty cold out here; let's go back inside."

"You go in. I'm going to sit out here for a bit longer, you know, think about everything you've told me."

51

"Well, if you're OK being alone, that's fine. But don't stay out too long."

Janet stooped down to kiss her daughter on the forehead and then headed back inside.

Emily stared up at the vast black cloak of a sky and spotted the seven stars of the Great Bear constellation, her mind trying to take in all she had just been told. Answers to so many questions were now slotting into place. Of course she couldn't stray from the paths or touch the fence or anger her boss enough to provoke her into pressing the emerald. And what about Lady Grubnot's vile behaviour towards her own doting parents and the way the royal family had banished her? Then of course there was the constant sniping at her and Paul for being "filthy little children". It didn't take a genius to work out where that hatred came from. And Emily's poor dad; Monty couldn't have known that it was all a trick – the offer Lady Grubnot outlined sounded incredibly good.

Reams of new information had been crammed into Emily's head over a very short space of time, like a dry well suddenly being flooded by cool, fresh water. First meeting Zak and all of his talk about the outside world, and now her mum's revelations about the history of how they got here. It had been an utterly remarkable series of events. What Emily wasn't to know at this stage though was that the days ahead would be much, much more remarkable.

CHAPTER NINE
MR PROUDFOOT
AND THE PETRUCIS

We must now, for a short while, turn our attentions away from Emily, Lady Grubnot and the appalling conditions of her workers, and shine the spotlight on another crisp-making establishment, this one situated on an industrial unit on the mainland, some forty miles or so from Grubnot Island.

It was here at 7.03 a.m. the following morning that Michael and Sonia Petruci were walking towards the loading bay behind their small Potato Ovals snack factory, when they spied a man standing next to the closed steel shutters that led inside. His most distinguishing feature was his large potbelly, for it protruded quite some distance over his belt line, but he also had a fleshy bulbous nose and ruddy cheeks. He was carrying a black briefcase with large gold locks, and a thick grey file.

Like Lady Grubnot, the Petrucis operated at the "posh" end of the crisp market and, similar to her output, their packets were expensive (although nowhere near as expensive as hers). It was here, however, that the similarities ended. While Lady Grubnot treated her workforce with rancour and contempt, the Petrucis treated their workers with respect and kindness, and paid them well above the market rate.

"Mr and Mrs Petruci?" enquired the man.

"Yes," replied Sonia as she and Michael strolled over to him.

"Arthur Proudfoot from IPSRA – the International Potato Snack Regulatory Association," he replied, shaking their hands and giving his business card to Sonia who looked at it and passed it over to Michael.

"How can we help you, Mr Proudfoot?" asked Sonia, smiling to herself about a large Danish order that had come in the day before.

"I assume you got IPSRA notice R179?" asked Mr Proudfoot, blinking a couple of times.

Michael looked blank. Sonia shook her head.

A dark blue truck from the ladder-making company next door cruised past the loading bay and its driver, a young bearded man, gave the Petrucis a wave.

"It was sent to all potato snack manufacturers a month or so ago," added Mr Proudfoot. "It concerned inspections within the industry."

"We fall under the local council," replied Michael. "Their health and safety team carried out a full inspection three months ago and we passed with flying colours."

"That's excellent!" Mr Proudfoot smiled. "But as of last month, in addition to local council inspections, all potato-snack producers must also be inspected by IPSRA. The paperwork's all contained in here."

He handed Sonia the thick grey file. She opened it and saw that it was crammed with documents. She and her husband flicked through letters, memos and minutes from meetings, on headed notepaper from the House of Commons, the Ministry of Agriculture, Fisheries and Food, and the Health and Safety Executive, to name but three.

"So when are IPSRA going to carry out their inspection?" asked Sonia.

"Why, right now!" Mr Proudfoot beamed. "I have all the necessary paperwork and tools in here." He patted his briefcase. "And as your local council gave you such a clean bill of health I imagine I'll be in and out pretty sharpish. Shall we...?" He indicated the steel shutters.

"Of course." Sonia smiled, unlocking three padlocks and lifting the shuttered door up and open. "Let's go inside."

They walked in and Michael pressed a panel of switches on the wall. The small factory was suddenly bathed in light. Unlike Lady Grubnot's set-up, all of the machinery and tools here were shiny, safe and serviced by industry professionals on a regular basis. The place carried a scent of rock salt mixed with mild disinfectant, a not too unpleasant-smelling combination.

Mr Proudfoot opened his briefcase on a spotless white surface and withdrew a red clipboard with a checklist attached. Under the watchful eyes of the Petrucis, he examined the various bright and clean sections of the production process and found each to be more than satisfactory. He was reaching out to tick the last item on his checklist, when he stopped and frowned. He leant forward to take a closer look at a thin army- green pipe on the wall and pulled a small, square black digital reader out of his briefcase.

"Is everything OK?" asked Sonia.

Mr Proudfoot didn't reply. Instead he held his reader up against the pipe and it buzzed. He shook his head gravely.

"What is it?' asked Michael.

He and Sonia hurried over to the inspector, anxious but not panicking.

"I'm afraid we have a problem," said Mr Proudfoot. He pointed with his pen to the green pipe. It was a waste pipe that snaked across the wall above the conveyor belt that carried the potatoes to the de-starching area. Michael and Sonia followed his pen and saw to their horror that a section of the pipe had split and was letting out a small drop of fluid every thirty seconds or so.

"That…that's not possible," whispered Sonia, aghast.

Mr Proudfoot placed his reader at the open mouth of the pipe and it buzzed again, while two red digital words appeared on its front. He turned it round so that the Petrucis could see them: SALMONELLA DETECTED.

Michael staggered backwards and Sonia had to put her arm out to stop him toppling over. Salmonella is of course a bacterium that when eaten can cause severe and even deadly food poisoning. In simple terms, it's not very good for you. In more complicated terms, it can kill you.

Mr Proudfoot was white in the face and looked as disturbed as the Petrucis.

"But we check the pipework at least twice a week," Sonia managed to croak. "I looked over it on Friday. It was in perfect shape. We're incredibly hot on safety here."

"I am so sorry." Mr Proudfoot grimaced. "But salmonella has been detected in your production line and a protocol established by ISPRA and the Health and Safety Executive must now be followed."

"What protocol?" asked Sonia, terrified of the answer.

"For a start you will have to take out adverts in every national and many of the regional newspapers informing the public that you are recalling every packet of crisps that has left this factory since the local council inspection three months ago."

"That's thousands, no, tens of thousands of packets," whispered a stunned Michael.

"Secondly, you will also need to stage a complete overhaul of your manufacturing process."

"It'll cost a fortune," said Sonia, a pain rising in her chest, her hands feeling hot and sticky.

"If placing the adverts and rebuilding the factory will place too great a financial strain on you, there is an alternative," said Mr Proudfoot.

"What alternative?" asked Michael.

"You could have a fire sale: sell everything, including responsibility for the huge costs I've outlined, to a third party such as another crisp manufacturer."

"But it's taken us seven years to build this business," groaned Sonia. "Selling it on would be a tragedy."

"Tragedy or not," said Mr Proudfoot, "I do think it might be the right way forward in this most difficult situation."

There was silence for a few moments as the staggering power of this information punched away at the Petrucis. It was Michael who managed to regain the benefit of speech first.

"But we don't know any other manufacturers to sell to," he said. "We wouldn't know where to start."

"I'm sure I can be of some assistance in this matter," replied Mr Proudfoot. "I have an extensive network of contacts in the industry and, with your permission, I will get on to them right away. If you get an offer from another crisp company, I suggest you take it and then try to start another business in a totally new field. You've proven you can run this enterprise successfully; I'm sure you will prosper in your new area of choice."

"Either way, this is a nightmare," muttered Sonia, her haggard face oozing despair.

"I really am so very sorry," said Mr Proudfoot, sighing heavily and looking like he was about to start crying. "I can't stand situations such as these where good, honest people are dealt such a terrible blow."

The Petrucis stood huddled together, unable to move as they watched Mr Proudfoot walk under the shutters. With a heavy step he marched away, rounding the corner of the loading bay and disappearing from view.

In just twenty minutes, their entire world had been shattered.

CHAPTER TEN
ZAK'S IDEA

For the rest of that week Emily did all of her usual things. She worked with her dad at the frying station, she played chess with her granddad, she took her turns cooking and cleaning and tidying the shack. But all the while her mind kept shunting back to two vital questions: first, might she get to see Zak again on Saturday; and second, now that she knew about her life situation and how it came about, was there any chance she would ever be able to get her family and friends to see and experience the world beyond Grubnot Island?

When close of play on Saturday finally arrived, Emily was the first person out of the production-room door after being paid, in this case with a small battered onion.

"Can you give us a hand with some laundry back home?" asked Janet, catching up with her as they neared the fork in the path.

"Sorry, Mum," replied Emily, handing Janet the onion, and trying to look composed enough to hide the excitement she was feeling within her. "But I just want to walk and get some fresh air."

"We can hang the laundry outside, that's fresh air."

"I know, it's just that I've...I've got a bit of a headache and I want to be alone for a bit."

Janet gave her daughter a quizzical look but before she could ask any further questions, Emily said, "See you later," turned onto the left path and walked away calmly.

"Don't stray from the paths!" called Janet.

Emily raised her hand in acknowledgement of this warning and, when she was out of sight, she increased her pace until she was running, all the while preparing herself for great disappointment.

Maybe Zak won't be with Mr Faraday today – he might be ill.

Or maybe he will be with Mr Faraday but he won't have time to come and see me.

Or maybe he thought I was weird for not knowing about school and he won't want to see me.

Or maybe he's an agent of Lady Grubnot and he's already reported back to her on our conversation last week.

Emerging from the thicket of oak trees, she came upon the hidden path and, after a quick check that all in the vicinity was quiet, she began her bush-busting antics once more and made it up to the fence. She could feel her body buzzing with excitement as she crouched down and peered through the hole, terrified of getting a vicious electric shock. There was the grassy slope and the vast expanse of water beyond it, but there was no sign of Zak.

Be patient, she told herself, *you're a bit earlier than you were last week.* She spent five minutes crouching down and looking through the hole but there were no developments on the other side. Five minutes later she was beginning to feel the dark depths of disappointment she'd tried to prepare herself for. She turned away from the fence and sat down miserably, unsure what to do next. Where was the boat? There couldn't be any deliveries without Mr Faraday. And because he was late Zak would probably have no time to come and see her even if he wanted to. After a further five minutes she was preparing to leave when she heard the distant sound of a boat engine and soon after that an eye appeared by the hole.

"ZAK!" she exclaimed when she crouched down and her eye met his. "Don't touch the fence."

"I won't!" he replied.

Today he was dressed in jeans, a plain red T-shirt and black trainers.

"Mr Faraday had to do something with one of his sons so we're a bit late today," panted Zak. "I sneaked off because he started some big conversation with Clemence about fishing."

"I'm so glad you made it," said Emily.

"I've been thinking about what you told me last week," went on Zak, "you know, about not knowing what a school is and the way you have to work for mouldy vegetable payments and all of that. Is it all really true? Because if it's not, I'd like you to tell me now and not make a fool out of me."

"It's all true. I'm not making fun of you. Now please tell me more about that school place and the things you do there."

"Well, school starts at nine a.m.," sighed Zak. "That's when the teachers do this thing called the register; it's just a list of all of the kids who should be there. When your name's read out you say yes and the teacher ticks your name off. It's a way of making sure no one's bunking off – that's hanging around by the sweet shop or going to the park to play football with your friends."

"What do they teach you?"

"In the morning we do English and maths. English is OK because you can sometimes write stories. You have to do spelling as well which is a total pain. I'm rubbish at it. Maths can be fun if we learn by playing games and doing number experiments. When it's straight from a book it's beyond boring."

"What about the afternoons?"

"We do art or games or music. At least that's the way it is in my school. After the summer holidays I'm going to another school for older kids."

"It all sounds wonderful," gasped Emily.

"It's not *that* good. I haven't told you about detentions and exams and Mr Arbuthnot who gives us French tests all the time and shouts like an angry chicken."

Emily laughed as Zak gave her a quick, head-tutting cockerel impression.

"What do you do when you're not in school and when you're not working for Mr Faraday?" She was so eager to glean information she was speaking at a ridiculously rapid pace.

"At the weekends I like to ride my bike, go and see films and play baseball with my mates."

"Films?" asked Emily.

Zak scratched his head. "They're these moving pictures that tell a story on a screen. There are all different types: sci-fi, thrillers, comedies."

Emily had heard there was some kind of viewing machine called a "TV" in Lady Grubnot's study but she'd never seen it. Films were also a mystery, but they sounded fun. "Do you have brothers and sisters?" she asked.

"Nah, there's only me. I *do* have loads of cousins and we all live really close to each other. Some are old, some are young. The older ones have jobs. Mike works in a curtain shop, Jeanie runs a toyshop, and Charlie, who's my age and looks like me, is more like a brother than a cousin. He works up at Farham Castle on the catering side. But enough about me, I want to talk about you and your life on this crummy island. You're really telling me that you're all locked away here, working all of those hours just to line Lady Grubnot's pockets? You should be out on the mainland living a normal life!"

"My first year and a half was spent off the island but I don't remember anything about it. Being here is the only thing I've ever known."

"Are there any other kids in there?"

"There's just Paul. He's nine."

"How many of you are there altogether?"

"Seven, including me, my parents and my granddad."

"And you all live in the manor house?"

"As if! We live in a rickety wooden shack and use bark to make our bowls and cutlery."

"This gets worse!" gasped Zak. "It's outrageous. Why don't you just leave?"

"It's impossible," sighed Emily. "Away from the main paths, the whole estate is littered with unexploded bombs. The fence is wired with explosives and has a vicious electrical current running through it. That's why we must never touch it."

"No way!"

"Plus Lady Grubnot wears an emerald pendant round her neck that has a switch to set everything off at the same time. She'd prefer to blow herself and all of us up rather than let us escape."

"An explosive emerald pendant! This is appalling! You've got to fight back."

"How can we fight when we know it's a losing battle? At the first sign of trouble she'll obliterate us all."

Zak stood up and started pacing around in small circles, deep in thought. "We'll think of something to get you all out of there," he said firmly. "But before we come up with the big, island-busting plan, you can start with a *psychological* war."

"A what?"

"You've got to get under Lady Grubnot's skin – annoy her, make her uneasy, soften her up for the main attack."

"How do I do that?"

"You play mind games with her."

"I'm afraid I don't know any games like that. We've only got chess and draughts here."

"No, it's not a game like that, it's something stealthy and subtle; something invisible to the naked eye and inaudible to the naked ear; something that'll rattle her. You've got to wind her up, make her question her own sanity."

"Let me get this straight," said Emily, hoping she'd understood. "You think I should do something that irritates or upsets her and, in doing so, weakens her a little, but do it in such a way that she doesn't know I'm doing it."

"Spot on!" Zak nodded. "Something small but, in its own way, something powerful. You don't have to do it all in one go. You can do it in stages, with each act seemingly unconnected to the next. I reckon it's all you can do at this stage, without getting the entire island smashed to pieces. Will any of the others be able to help you out with this?"

"I don't want anyone else involved," said Emily. "The adults would forbid me from taking any action, I'm sure of it, and Paul is…a bit young. I think I'm going to have to do this by myself."

"Fine," replied Zak, "but don't take any risks. This has to be a very clever operation. If you can unnerve her, she'll be a little less strong when we really take her on. It's the kind of game countries play with each other before they start an all-out war."

"Like Pirate Summers and the rooftop shouting match with Old Purple."

"What are you talking about?"

"It doesn't matter, I'm just trying to prepare myself."

"Oh, there's something else," said Zak. He reached into his pocket, pulled out a green tube with silver swirl patterns and pushed it through the hole. It landed on the ground and Emily picked it up. Tearing open the top she found a stack of ten small orange circles encrusted with sugar.

"They're called Sugar Shots," said Zak. "They're a type of sweet. Try one."

Hesitantly, Emily popped one of the orange discs into her mouth and her face transformed into a look of pure joy. It was incredible! So sweet and tangy! Unlike anything else she'd ever tasted. She chewed in rapturous delight.

"Do you like it?" asked Zak.

"Like it?" exclaimed Emily. "I LOVE it! Thank you SO much."

"At least it isn't crisps," said Zak.

Emily refrained from telling Zak that she actually loved crisps and instead reached for another Sugar Shot. But at that moment she heard a chilling voice cut through the early evening air, like a deadly scythe.

"Clemence, what's that by the fence? I'm sure I just saw something moving."

CHAPTER ELEVEN
THE GIRL VANISHES

Emily was flat on her face on the ground in less than a second, praying that she hadn't been spotted.

"I'm not sure," answered Clemence, who was dressed in his estate manager outfit of green corduroy trousers, green jacket and sturdy brown boots. "It was most probably a rabbit."

"What's going on?" demanded Zak through the fence.

"Shhhh!" hissed Emily. "It's *her*!"

"That was no rabbit, you idiot – it was bigger, I'm sure of it."

Emily felt her insides squash together as if they were little kids trying to hide behind a narrow pillar in the face of a terrifying beast.

"Maybe a fox then," opined Clemence.

"No, you buffoon, it wasn't orange!"

The two of them were now a very short distance from the beginning of the overgrown path.

Emily was convinced that if Lady Grubnot spotted the path she would investigate it.

"She's vile!" snarled Zak, his tone dripping with disgust.

"Shhhhhhh!" Emily implored him again.

"I heard a sound?" snapped Lady Grubnot, her angular features fixed on the portion of fence below which Emily was hiding.

"I've got to go," said Zak.

"Wait," pleaded Emily, in a state of terror. If Lady Grubnot found her she'd probably throw her straight onto the fence and frazzle her to an electric soup. *Maybe I should make a dash for it – crawl away through the dense bushes, while hoping I don't make the acquaintance of any explosives?*

"Maybe it was a stray dog," suggested Clemence.

"How on earth could a dog get onto the island?!" shouted Lady Grubnot.

"Just wait a bit," whispered Emily, "there's so much more to talk about."

"Sorry, but Mr Faraday needs me," said Zak, turning and sprinting away.

"Wait here a moment, Clemence," ordered Lady Grubnot. She took a few steps forward until the front of her shoes were touching the leaves Emily had lain on the ground to conceal her path.

Lady Grubnot sniffed the air and narrowed her eyes. Her head swivelled from side to side like a remote-controlled CCTV camera. Her angular features protruded outwards, threatening to leave her face and conduct an investigation by themselves.

Emily was frozen rigid, unable to move, unable to think.

Lady Grubnot was about to crouch down and move these leaves aside when Clemence suddenly commanded her attention. "Your TV programme begins shortly," he said hastily. "The one about the con artist who cheated members of the royal family."

"What of it?" asked Lady Grubnot, hovering over the leaves.

"It starts in fifteen minutes. Apparently the criminal took a massive chunk of their cash reserves. But it didn't just cost them money, it dented their pride as well."

Lady Grubnot paused; whenever a nugget of humiliation was dished out to the royal family, she wanted to see it. She craved opportunities such as this, revelling in any discomfort the royals felt.

"I was reminded of the time by my soon-to-be-patented wearable ear alerter," said Clemence proudly, tapping a tiny green receiver plugged into his left ear. "Can I show you its multiple capabilities?"

Lady Grubnot spun round and eyed Clemence with fury.

"No, Clemence, you may not show me its capabilities. I do not wish to see, hear or be made aware of any of your ridiculous inventions, so kindly SHUT UP about them. Now let's hurry up. I'm eager to see any royal personages squirming."

A moment later they were hurrying back in the direction of the manor house, Lady Grubnot striding purposefully, Clemence rushing at her side, trying to interest her in the new soon-to-be-patented breakfast cereal capsules he was working on. "They fight off hunger for three whole days," he informed her enthusiastically.

She growled at him and started walking faster.

Emily stayed rigidly still for ten minutes until all sound and sight of Lady Grubnot and Clemence had vanished. When she finally did decide to move and head for home, in her mouth she chewed another Sugar Shot, while in her mind she chewed over Zak's fascinating proposition.

CHAPTER TWELVE
THE SOON-TO-BE-PATENTED ELECTRIC BOOST STILTS

On Sunday the sun shone as if it intended to bathe the whole word in a yellowy orange sheen, a distant but proud circle, balancing perfectly in an azure sky. After a leisurely breakfast of nuts and berries that they'd picked, Emily and Paul went for a stroll and ended up playing catch with a manky old ball they'd found in a ditch the summer before.

Emily wasn't exactly bored but she was losing enthusiasm for this pursuit when they heard a crashing sound nearby. Paul dropped the ball and they raced round the corner to discover the source of the noise.

There was Clemence, in a crumpled heap on the ground, his limbs caught up in two red metal sticks. Near the bottom of each was a sticking-out oval rubber surface, about the size of a large apple's circumference.

"Would you mind giving me a hand?" asked Clemence, sounding a little ashamed. Paul untangled his limbs from the metal, while Emily, using all of her strength, dragged Clemence to his feet. She looked around to see if Lady Grubnot was in the area. Of the cruel and bitter tyrant there was no sign.

"What are you doing?" asked Emily.

Clemence sighed the sigh of an inventor with too many ideas in his head but not enough practical acumen to bring them to life. "These are my new soon-to-be-patented electric boost stilts."

"What are stilts?" asked Paul.

Clemence picked up the red sticks, placed his left foot on the rubber platform of one stilt, and his right on the platform of the other. He swayed precariously for a few moments and then began walking, or wobbling in this case. He made it a couple of metres but then teetered so violently he had to jump off or risk another calamitous fall.

"How are they *electric*?" asked Emily.

Clemence laid the stilts on the ground and crouched down beside them. Carefully, he unscrewed a silver cap at the bottom of one stilt and a sprawling mess of green, red and blue wires spilled out.

"If the electrical power worked properly these would be easier to walk on and would theoretically allow the user to leap off the ground. Unfortunately I haven't quite got the technicalities correct."

He played with the wires for a minute or so but then cursed under his breath.

"Er…would you mind me taking a look?" asked Emily.

Clemence looked up at her and his lips quivered. "Are you some kind of inventor too?" he asked, a tiny spark of hope igniting in his eyes.

"She can make anything," said Paul, his shoulders rising proudly like two sentries called to attention. "She's a real genius."

"Well then, be my guest." Clemence smiled. "Any technical assistance is always much appreciated."

Emily knelt down and examined the wires. She separated a few and looked at the small white panel they were attached to inside the stilt. "You don't happen to have a screwdriver do you?" she asked.

"In fact I do," replied Clemence, pulling one out of his jacket pocket and handing it over.

Emily undid some screws that were holding the wires to the panel and switched some of them to different positions. She then twisted back the metal cap, got off the ground and stood the stilts upright.

"Do you think that might have done it?" asked Clemence.

"I don't know," said Emily, holding out the stilts for him. "Why don't you try them and see."

"No," replied Clemence, shaking a finger. "You were bold enough to attempt a repair job, so you can have the first go."

"Really?" gasped Emily, unsure if she'd heard him correctly.

He nodded encouragingly.

Emily placed her hands near the top of the stilts, readied herself, and jumped onto the black rubber platforms.

She fell off instantly.

On her second attempt she didn't even get both feet on before she stumbled off. Goes three and four were no better. Emily, however, was one of the

world's most determined characters and on her fifth
go she took a few small steps. Then the stilts started
shaking. This shake quickly became a rumble and a
second later the stilts shot Emily a good two metres
in the air. They hit the ground and bounced, this
time launching her even higher.

"This is INCREDIBLE!" she shouted, the stilts
whooshing her three metres into the air, crashing
down and propelling her up again.

"I can almost see the tops of those trees!" she
called out, shooting up to a height of about six
metres, her stomach dipping and rising in time with
the automatic leg gadgets. It felt almost like flying.

"How do I turn them off?" she shouted, turning
round when she realised that the heights she was
reaching might make her visible to Lady Grubnot,
who would not be best pleased at her and Paul
fraternising with Clemence.

"There's a lever on the side of the left one!"
called up Clemence.

As Emily began her next descent, she located
the lever and pressed it. The stilts stopped buzzing,
reduced their speed and allowed her to make a rea-
sonably comfortable landing.

"I want a go, I want a go!" trilled Paul.

Emily passed him the stilts and following a few
unsuccessful tries Paul shot into the air too. Shortly
after, though, Clemence was reminded of the time
by his soon-to-be-patented wearable ear alerter and
asked Paul to return to solid ground.

"Sorry," said Clemence, quickly taking the stilts back. "I've got to rush. I need to get a souffle in the oven."

"Shame," groaned Paul, his face indicating he woud have liked a much longer go.

"Excellent work." Clemence nodded briskly to Emily, before using the stilts to make a bouncy, accident-filled journey back to the manor house.

Emily watched him go, her mind alive with possibilities. As well as meeting Zak and learning the true story of how she'd arrived here, she'd now had her first proper chat with Clemence and had helped him fix one of his crazy, soon-to-be-patented inventions. Maybe he or one of his gadgets might be able to help *her* at some stage?

CHAPTER THIRTEEN
THE CUNNING CRISP PLANS
OF LADY GRUBNOT

The sun was drifting away lazily behind a cloud and a chill wind was making an appearance as Emily and Paul headed back to the shack.

"That was amazing," said Paul, "although I wish I'd had a longer go."

"I'm sure there'll be another chance to try them out." Emily smiled. "Clemence seems kind and willing to share his creations."

"He's also a bit crazy," said Paul.

"His craziness is his best feature," said Emily. "That's probably soon-to-be-patented too."

Paul laughed. "Race you back!" he shouted, haring ahead.

As Emily, Paul and their families started supper that night in the shack and the island was bathed in darkness, up at the manor house, Lady Grubnot sipped a night-time drop of whisky in her study on the third floor.

The decor of the room hadn't been changed in fifty years. It boasted tasteful light-blue wallpaper, plush velvet curtains in purple, a long red chaise longue and a tatty green sofa against the wall facing a huge mahogany writing table on the other side of the room. This had three draws with an inkwell on the left. It was at this table that Lady Grubnot sat, allowing the whisky to swirl around in her glass like a breaking amber wave, before glugging it down and feeling the liquor ignite her insides.

Her mind turned – as it so often did in this study, once the study of her father, Fortescue – to the manner in which her treacherous parents had thrown away such vast sums of money to needy children dressed in rags. Every time she saw those two repulsive brats who worked in her crisp-production room – Emily and Paul – it reminded her of all those filthy little charity receptacles. Her parents hadn't been very charitable to *her*, had they? How much more cash she would have had if only they'd kept her in their wills, like normal parents, and given her what was rightfully hers? Such child neglect was monstrous. In her opinion, it should be made illegal. Who knows, if they'd left her a decent wedge she might have never needed to start her crisp-making operation, an operation that so exhausted her even though the actual work she did was on the micro side of minuscule.

And how could they have turned the royal family against her? She was an heir to the throne just like her father, but she'd received a lifetime ban on any involvement with the royals, and all on account of the fact that she'd had the odd tantrum at a palace or two, broken some worthless artefacts and attacked a few people. What was the big deal? She'd just been showing her strong personality and strength of character. The royal family despised her so much that when she announced she would be making crisps they'd made a public declaration that they would never, ever allow any of her snack foods within a hundred miles of them or the properties they owned. How mean-spirited and pathetically low they had stooped.

The cauldron of fury rose in her chest and she grabbed a heavy silver paperweight, shaped like a gambling chip, and hurled it towards the fireplace. On impact it smashed into thousands of splinters that cascaded down onto the tattered carpet.

But hang on a moment, Lady Grubnot told herself, pushing away the hate-stuffed bile for a moment. Wasn't she the one who had turned her parents' grotty crisp-production room into a colossally successful business? Wasn't it her who'd been lauded as one of the nation's finest and most shrewd business-women and had had her photo on the front pages of numerous business and financial magazines and web-sites? Wasn't she the one who reeled in gargantuan sums of money each and every day? Of course she was. Forget her beastly parents and the repugnant children they wasted their money on for a minute. It was time to celebrate her genius! She leant back in the chair and bathed in luxurious thoughts about the methods and strategies she had created and followed – paths that had opened the cash tills and never let them stop ringing. Her outgoings were minimal while her incomings were vast. That was the way to run a company; this was the way to become a legend.

As soon as she decided to make crisps commercially, Lady Grubnot vowed to shun the mainstream market. Her crisps would not be for the supermarket shelves and the ugly "plebs" who shovelled them into their mouths as quick as their malnourished fingers could manage. No. Her crisps would be for the "high-end" market, for the people who had stacks of money and wanted to vaunt their wealth. She read articles and studied sales figures, looked into the main industry players and the key movers and shakers in the upmarket snack world. After much thought, she named her crisps Grubnot's *Exclusive*, to give consumers an air of sophistication and "otherness". She had slick upmarket foil packets made and adorned these with words like "extravagant" and "opulent". She selected a rare breed of potatoes called Medlock that were only produced by one farmer. After a couple of trial runs (she had to do these herself because there was no point in grabbing a workforce if the set-up didn't work), she was delighted to discover the equipment her parents had purchased, although not in the best state of repair, worked perfectly well.

Cutting the potatoes into 1.2 millimetre slices and using the flavouring secrets her father had bought from Spud Murphy, the first ever batch of crisps she produced met with her instant approval. They made every other crisp she'd ever eaten taste stodgy and unpalatable. She was onto something; she knew she was. She was going to make the finest crisps the world had ever savoured and she would prove her greatness; a greatness that would place her above other mere mortals, and that included those despicable royals.

She chose flavours that were sure to attract the wealthy and from the start she charged outrageous prices. Thus Grubnot's Exclusive Oyster & Crushed Sea Salt flavour cost £10 a pack. Smoked Salmon & Hand-Picked Dill would set you back £20. Wild Mushroom were £30, followed by Artichoke & Chilli (£40), then Stilton & Sundried Tomato (£50), Lobster & Tarragon (£60), moving on to Frogs' Legs & Peppered Olive Oil (£80), Champagne (£100), and finally, for the most expensive tastes, Foie Gras (£120) and Caviar Elite (£150).

These prices probably seem unbelievable, extravagant and outrageous to you, but very soon it became clear that people with lots of money like spending lots of money. It makes them feel good. They don't drive basic cars; they drive expensive low silver vehicles that look closer to spaceships than the ordinary A to B husks of metal you see on the highways and byways. They eat at restaurants with eye-watering prices, where all you're served is a cube of beetroot and a macadamia nut in a small dollop of pungent green sauce. After you've polished off these tiny morsels (which takes about three seconds) you're served a telephone-number bill that would give most diners an extreme case of heartburn and cash-burn. These people live in gated communities with teams of security guards to keep out anyone other than other exclusive types. Unsurprisingly, it's the same with snack foods. These people love to furnish their snack bowls with crisps unaffordable to ninety-nine per cent of the population. So Grubnot's Exclusive crisps had no shortage of paying customers.

And there was another equally astonishing element to the whole enterprise: in each packet of Grubnot's Exclusive crisps there were just ten crisps. That's right – *ten*. This meant that if you had enough money to buy a packet of Caviar Elite flavour, *each individual crisp* in that packet would set you back *a crisp £15*. Never before had there been crisps like these, with their mix of enticing flavours and sky-high price tags.

But Lady Grubnot had another couple of masterstrokes up her sleeve.

The first was that she did not sell her crisps to any middlemen or women, like shops, stores and cafés. The only way to get your hands on her crisps was by filling out an order form and posting it directly to Grubnot Island. Supermarkets and posh delicatessens pleaded with her to supply them but she stood firm. She insisted on controlling every aspect of the business so if anyone wanted her crisps they'd have to buy them from her.

The second was perhaps the cleverest wheeze of them all.

Customers could only purchase a maximum of *three packets per week*. No more and no exceptions.

Within days of opening for business it became clear that demand for Grubnot's Exclusive crisps wouldn't just outstrip supply, it would trample it down in a frenzied stampede, like wildebeest fleeing from a voracious lion or a young boy leaping away from an older sister, the sister from whom he has just stolen an entire week's pocket money.

The orders came flooding in, from Ballymena to Beirut, from Salisbury to South Africa, from Truro to Turkmenistan. On Monday and Thursday the postman steered his postal boat to the island and delivered sacks and sacks of order forms, mountains and forests of them, to the greedy hands of Lady Grubnot.

For a normal person, an order of three packs of Grubnot's crisps could well represent a week's salary or more, so it was mainly massive landowners and city lawyers, hedge-fund managers and banking titans, rich sports stars and celebrity chat-show hosts who could afford to purchase them. Not all rich people bought them though. As we've seen, the royal family – although filled with many crisp devotees – imposed a blanket ban on Grubnot's Exclusives. They bought *their* upmarket crisps from one of the other six "high-end" crisp manufacturers.

This maximum-packets rule was a marketing masterstroke and very early on it became quite clear that for some of her customers three weekly servings of Grubnot's Exclusives would not be enough. One rainy afternoon the Duke of Hazel-Norton (not a member of the royal family or an heir to the throne) navigated his way to Grubnot Island in a very agitated state with a vast packing case stuffed with fifty-pound notes. These he offered as an inducement to Lady Grubnot to allow him to purchase some extra packs of Lobster & Tarragon flavour because he had run out before the end of the week and was literally tearing his hair out in desperation for more. But Lady Grubnot sent the Duke away empty-handed.

The maximum order applied to everyone regardless, she told him in no uncertain terms. By the time the Duke made it back home, the unfortunate gentleman was completely bald.

Before long, word spread of the incredible taste and delicious texture of Grubnot's Exclusives and people outside of these very rich sets began to hanker after them too. If they didn't have that kind of money then they went and sought it out. There were reports of people borrowing vast sums of money and remortgaging their houses to buy packets, and in one case a perfectly respectable lollipop lady held up her local bank (disguised as a lollipop lady) with her lollipop stick just so she could get her hands on some extra cash to buy some of the hotly sought-after snacks. Unfortunately one of the bank tellers was the lollipop lady's sister so identifying her to the police was fairly straightforward. She received a lengthy prison sentence and her lollipop stick was confiscated. So instead of receiving any of Lady Grubnot's mouth-watering offerings she lay on her prison bed, dreaming each night that the circular top of her lollipop stick had turned into a giant Grubnot's crisp.

As soon as Lady Grubnot had kidnapped her workforce, she informed them that on each day, from Monday to Friday, they would produce 10,000 packets, 5,000 of one flavour and 5,000 of another, making a weekly total of 50,000. Even for the most extreme potato snack fan, that is a lot of crisps. With 200 packets in every box, this meant her workforce had to fill 250 boxes every week.

Emily and her co-workers then spent a large part of Saturday opening the thousands of order forms sent to the island and dividing the crisps into individually addressed packages, which were then placed in regional boxes, so the delivery drivers could deliver to their specific areas. The orders were fulfilled on a first come, first served basis – whichever order forms were opened first were completed. They did this until all 50,000 packs were accounted for. This led one customer – a leading financial advisor – to announce that after missing out for three weeks running, he would kill his daughter's Barbie doll live on TV if he didn't get any Grubnot's Exclusives in the fourth week. Luckily his name was picked that week and the doll was mercifully saved.

The figures involved in the business were staggering. With an average selling price of £66 per packet, Lady Grubnot took in around £3 million per week or £171 million per year, the kind of sums leading footballers can only drool over. In terms of her costs, she rewarded her workers with mouldy veg, got the lowest deal possible with the potato farmer and the foil-pack maker, and paid a pittance to Clemence, Mr Faraday and the lorry drivers. She kept gas and electricity bills very low by using miniscule amounts of heating and light and she adopted several schemes to avoid paying tax. By doing all of these unpleasant manoeuvres she was able to pocket nearly all of her turnover. She'd paid off her gambling debts within three months of starting production and she had no intention of stopping making crisps and raking in money until her dying breath. Her bank balance was so high that even she sometimes had difficulty appreciating how many millions it held.

As she bathed in the glory of her crisp-making endeavours, Lady Grubnot leant back in her study chair and thoughts of her "big" plan dropped into her mind – a plan that would put everything she'd achieved so far into the shade. It would soon fling her onto the front pages of every newspaper on earth. She would sweep from being a vastly wealthy and well-recognised business tycoon into someone feted by world leaders and whose name would ring out from radio, television and the multiple platforms of the internet. And the wonderful thing was, she wouldn't even have to leave Grubnot Island to achieve this goal.

She grabbed her walkie-talkie and barked at Clemence: "I'll have my sole fillets and lightly boiled potatoes in the study tonight, and when you come, bring a dustpan and brush."

"As you wish," replied Clemence, who was skidding over fish skins and olive oil on the kitchen floor.

And with that she grabbed her whisky glass and threw it towards the fireplace where on impact it smashed satisfyingly into hundreds of pieces.

Chapter Fourteen
A Small Act
of Subversion

As Emily began work the following day, Zak's latest words went skimming over the grooves and along the neural pathways of her brain.

You have to get under her skin, annoy her, make her uneasy.

It has to be stealthy and subtle; something invisible to the naked eye and inaudible to the naked ear.

She liked the idea behind his suggestion. Getting into Lady Grubnot's mind to weaken her a little was a good way of laying the ground for doing something greater, whatever that something may be. And within an hour, a small act of subversion was beginning to crystallise in her mind. As the day progressed, she went over her idea again and again, trying to figure out *when* she should launch her little scheme and *how* she could put it into practice without creating massive trouble for herself.

As the end of the working day loomed, with everyone sealing the Stilton & Sundried Tomato and Lobster & Tarragon crisps into their foil packets, Emily positioned herself at a worktop some distance away from the others. There was nothing unusual in this; people worked on sealing in all areas of the production room. But Emily wanted to work in this space because she didn't want anyone to hear what she was about to do. If someone cottoned onto her scheme, major complications would arise. Her mum and dad would most certainly start asking questions and demand an explanation for behaviour that was both provocative and dangerous.

Emily deliberately started working a tiny bit slower than the usual frantic pace Lady Grubnot demanded; not slow enough for any of the other workers to notice, but enough to grab Lady Grubnot's attention.

Before long the terror-inducing, clanking shoes started beating a path in Emily's direction and a few seconds later a spiteful hand grabbed her by the shoulder and spun her round.

"WHY HAVE YOU REDUCED YOUR WORK PACE, YOU FOUL CHILD?" yelled Lady Grubnot, glaring at Emily with fury. "Are you trying to make sure we don't bag the full ten thousand packs today? Do you think this is some kind of CHARITY for lazy, uncouth workers, is that it?"

It was then that Emily struck.

"Nop at all," she replied, a sincere and apologetic expression on her face, while her nerves tingled.

"What did you say?" snarled Lady Grubnot, leaning forward like a sinister, twisted lamp post.

"Not at all," said Emily, suddenly speeding up her work rate. She waited for a pinch or a slap or a smack but nothing was issued.

Lady Grubnot harrumphed irritably.

Emily kept her eyes on the crisp packets.

87

"You know full well how much I demand speed, you junior irritant," seethed the Lady. "Speed makes more crisps. More crisps make me more money."

"I promise I'll go baster," replied Emily.

Lady Grubnot scowled. "What did you say, child?" She turned her head so that her right ear was closer to Emily.

"I said I promise I'll go faster."

Lady Grubnot opened her mouth to shout something but then closed it again. She harrumphed once more. She put her fingers in her ears to see if there were any blockages. She shook her head. She stomped off.

Emily kept up her quickened work rate, a picture of honest toil and impeccable stamina.

Replacing one letter; that's all it had taken.

Not had become *nop*.

Faster had become *baster*.

The second time she'd said each word, she'd said it properly, and having pulled off this stunt she felt a small glow of pride light up inside her. Lady Grubnot had been irked; of that there was no doubt. And more importantly, Emily seemed to have got away with it.

What she'd just done wasn't earth-shattering, it wasn't epoch-making, but in its own way it represented a tiny victory, the start of what Zak had called the *psychological* battle. Emily realised she was looking a little bit satisfied so she quickly transformed her expression to one of standard misery before she finished sealing her current clutch of packets and went to get some more.

CHAPTER FIFTEEN
STRIKE TWO

Emboldened by the success of her first subversive act, Emily waited until Wednesday to try out another ruse.

In the late afternoon, Lady Grubnot glanced out of a window and spied Emily meandering back (and, unknown to the Lady, doing it on purpose) from the outdoor toilet. Snarling with rage, Lady Grubnot hurried outside and blocked Emily's path.

"A snail could move ten times faster than you!" shouted Lady Grubnot. "A two-toed sloth is a sprinter compared to you! What have I told you about loitering on your unnecessary breaks? My weekly orders must be completed!"

This time instead of *saying* anything, Emily leant her neck a few millimetres to the left. Now I don't know if you've ever seen this before, but in a conversation between two people, if one person does something like this, the other person tends to mirror it.

And that's exactly what Lady Grubnot did. She moved her head in the same way without knowing that she'd done it.

"I do apologise," said Emily, tilting her head another fraction.

Lady Grubnot's neck made the same movement.

It's working, thought Emily. *It's actually working.*

"I've a good mind to dock you your day's pay!" shrieked Lady Grubnot, as Emily's head and then hers moved down another notch.

"I'll double my work rate for the rest of the day," said Emily, daring to lower her head one last time.

"Well get on with it!" snapped Lady Grubnot, her head dipping again too.

And there the conversation stopped, with them both standing there like penguin puppets, their heads cocked to one side.

As Emily scurried back inside, Lady Grubnot noticed a sharp pang of pain in her neck but had no idea where it had come from. She straightened up and cricked her neck both ways. The pain remained. She stamped her foot in exasperation. She muttered the words "osteopath" and "craniologist". She massaged her neck on both sides and stamped her foot again.

"I'm fine!" she snapped to herself. "I'm not paying some quack doctor to pummel my neck and make it worse before issuing me with a gigantic bill and a next appointment. A good drop of whisky will cure this!"

And with that she stormed off to the manor house.

CHAPTER SIXTEEN
A PINCH OF PILFERING;
A SPECK OF SPYING

Buoyed by her two mini-triumphs and sure that Zak would be proud of her, Emily grabbed Paul as darkness fell the next day, and together they scurried towards the manor house for a little spot of filching. Emily glanced up and was reassured to see the constellation of Cepheus beaming down at her, its pencil-like outline a frame for its kingly image. They passed the large tarmac square at the front of the house, stole past a line of swaying beech trees, and crept round a snaking path leading to the back of the building.

Paul turned the kitchen door. "It's locked," he whispered.

Luckily for them, Lady Grubnot hadn't kept up the payments on the burglar alarm system her parents had installed many years ago. Why pay some bumbling fool to come and tinker with the sensors once a year at an exorbitant cost? And besides, there was no one on the island who would remotely think about breaking in.

"Let's try the windows," said Emily.

The second window they touched was open a fraction. Emily reached in, pulled it wide open and, using the sill to lift herself up, scrambled inside. Paul followed quickly.

The kitchen was dark and foreboding. The utensils and machines resembled a silent, cloaked army, awaiting instructions to attack.

They crept forward stealthily, knowing the route so well. After all, without their weekly pilfering visits to the manor house, Lady Grubnot's workers could have easily starved.

Past the old-fashioned and leaky fridge they went, round the ancient Aga cooker, along the panelled walls, right until they reached the pantry. Lady Grubnot spent the least possible amount she could on the groceries Mr Faraday delivered to the island, but she got just enough to make the kitchen breakins of Emily and Paul worthwhile.

Emily very slowly turned the pantry door and they scurried inside like two crumb-searching mice. The pantry was illuminated by a single shaft of moonlight that drifted in through a tiny barred window.

"OK," whispered Emily, opening the small backpack she'd brought with her. "Some fresh yeast, a tin of butter beans, a couple of slices of bread and some sprinkles of oregano."

She and Paul darted around collecting these and placed them in the backpack.

"How about some of these wheat crackers?" asked Paul, pointing to a packet that had already been opened.

Emily nodded and he dropped a couple in.

"OK," whispered Emily, "job done."

They started making their way back to the pantry door when a cardboard box on a high shelf caught Emily's eye: BERKSHIRE CRISPS it read on the side. Emily felt her taste buds spring to attention. Berkshire Crisps. This could be the chance to taste a second and maybe third crisp. It was sorely tempting. But then she frowned. Why would Lady Grubnot need to buy crisps from another company when she had so many produced right here on the island?

"Maybe she wants to know what the competition tastes like," suggested Paul, reading Emily's thoughts.

Emily nodded. If the box was full of Berkshire Crisp packets she would take one and hope that Lady Grubnot wouldn't be counting them. But to Emily's disappointment, when she checked the box she discovered it was empty.

"Or maybe Clemence likes Berkshires better than Grubnot's Exclusives. Maybe he secretly eats them in here so as not to be caught by her. There might have only been a couple of packets in the box."

They stood there for a few seconds, the moon lighting up their faces, before Emily nodded and they left the pantry to head back to the window. They were almost there when several voices sounded in the corridor outside. They froze, fearing the people behind the voices would enter the kitchen and see them instantly, thieves in their midst: robbers, burglars, criminals. But they didn't. The people carried on talking in the hallway for about thirty seconds and then opened the doors of the manor house's great hall and stepped in there, shutting the doors behind them.

One of the voices was Lady Grubnot's but Emily didn't recognise the others. Who could the Lady be talking to? No one ever came to the manor house, not even Mr Faraday and certainly not the postman; he delivered the crisp orders straight to the production room. So who were these visitors and what were they doing here? Emily was intrigued.

"Take the stuff and go back to the shack," she said to Paul, making a snap decision. She passed him the backpack.

"What are you going to do?" asked Paul.

"I'm just going to hang back and see what's going on out there."

"Can't I stay too?"

Emily shook her head. "It's better if I do it alone. Hiding one person is easier than hiding two. I won't stay too long, I promise. I just want to listen in for a bit."

"Fine," said Paul, a touch sulkily, "I'll wait up for you."

"Thanks." Emily nodded. "I'm sure I won't be long and I'll tell you what they're talking about if I can get close enough to hear them."

She waited until Paul had scampered back to the window and climbed out successfully before she made her move. Creeping along the walls, she opened the kitchen door and peered out.

The darkened corridor was empty. An oil painting of a man on a horse gazed out from a faded green wall. An ancient wooden bench with a leg missing was propped up against a wall, like an unevenly weighted monument about to topple over.

Emily waited a few seconds and, satisfied that the rumble of voices was definitely coming from the great hall, she darted into the breakfast room. She was well aware that inside the breakfast room there was an old wooden hatch that opened out onto the great hall. It must have been used for serving food in the past.

Woodworm and time had eaten away at this hatch and there was a small crack down its centre that allowed you to look from one room to the other. She'd spied through it a few times in the past as Lady Grubnot paced the great hall, yelling at Clemence for his poor cooking or screeching at suppliers for their disgraceful requests to up their prices a little.

Pressing her eye against the hatch crack, Emily looked through. The only light in the hall came from the reds and oranges of a crackling fire. The long dark brown curtains hung like funeral quilts and the polished wooden floorboards creaked whenever anyone rearranged their footing.

In addition to Lady Grubnot, three strangers – one woman and two men – were also in the hall. They were sitting at one end of the large oak dining table, while Lady Grubnot stood with her back to the fireplace, her features silhouetted and extended to even greater lengths by the long shadows the flames created. She eyed her guests with a dash of disdain and a haughty brow.

"I'm Arthur Proudfoot," stated one of the men. "We spoke on the telephone yesterday."

To Emily, this Mr Proudfoot looked a bit perturbed and a bit determined. He was stroking his rotund belly with one hand.

"You said on the phone you represent something called BIPSA?" said Lady Grubnot, gazing at him with a contemptuous frown.

"It's IPSRA," replied Proudfoot. "It stands for the International Potato Snack Regulatory Association."

"IPSRA, IPBA, IGGLER – they're all just stupid acronyms people invent to make themselves look important, to puff out their professional chests, don't you think, Mr Proudfoot?"

"No I do not," he said, clearly aggrieved by this insult. "My organisation was established to protect crisp manufacturers and their consumers. We have legal responsibilities. We might even be able to help *you* someday. So I would very much appreciate it if you didn't speak ill of it."

"As you wish," snapped Lady Grubnot, turning her hawkish gaze onto the other man and the woman. "And these are?"

"This is Sonia and Michael Petruci," said Proudfoot. "They are highly respected members of our industry who have a blemish-free track record and a highly profitable crisp business. They have won several awards and their small workforce is highly motivated and dedicated."

"And yet they are in some sort of trouble," said Lady Grubnot, narrowing her eyes and staring at the Petrucis with a searing glare. "Otherwise they wouldn't be here."

Mr Proudfoot coughed and mopped his brow with a handkerchief he pulled out of his jacket pocket. "Unfortunately there was a small issue when I made a regulatory inspection of their factory."

"With that issue being?"

"Traces of salmonella were detected in their production line."

The Petrucis looked at the floor in shame.

"Salmonella?" repeated the Lady, sneeringly blowing the word into the air like a horse snorting.

"It was a limited outbreak and occurred over a small surface area, but it means that they must follow certain industry protocols and in their long-term interests we feel it is probably best for them to sell the company to another crisp manufacturer who will be able to use their refurbished workspace to up-scale their own production."

Emily studied the Petrucis' faces. They looked utterly exhausted and dejected.

"In other words, both your brand and your products have been tainted beyond reach," said Lady Grubnot, a cruel smile playing on her face, her shadow seeming to independently sneak this way and that on the fading wallpaper.

"We've spoken to our workers and, although they are devastated by the situation, they've all declared their willingness to work for a new owner," said Sonia. "They are loyal and conscientious and would be an asset to any company."

"Our machinery is in excellent condition," added Michael. "After a thorough clean-up we're confident it will bring you large amounts of extra revenue. Plus, by buying us out you will also enable us to begin again in another industry and get back on our feet."

Michael Petruci sounded like he had practised this speech. When it was complete, a faint glimmer of hope attached itself to his and his wife's faces.

"I immediately thought of you, Lady Grubnot," said Proudfoot. "I am familiar with your company history and impressive sales figures. I like your business model. You know what it's like to build a business from scratch, just like the Petrucis have done. You should therefore be able to understand their dilemma and how much this all means to them. I feel it would be a wise move for you to take on their company and expand your production at their site. The extra profits you'd achieve could be huge."

He reached into his trouser pocket, pulled out a piece of paper, stood up and walked over to hand it to Lady Grubnot.

"This is the sort of figure we're looking for," he said.

Lady Grubnot snatched the paper from his hand and studied it as if it were a mythical beast about to attack her with its fearsome claws. She tutted several times and shook her head dismissively, in the manner a nursery teacher would to a child who has just spilled a beaker of water on her lap. Reaching into her jacket pocket, she withdrew a pen and crossed out several figures before handing the paper back to Mr Proudfoot.

"And this is the sort of figure I would be looking for," she declared, her face lit up in the poor light like an electric genie.

Even though Emily had seen countless outbursts and rages from Lady Grubnot, tonight in the sinister light of the great hall she looked even crueller than ever.

On seeing her slashed number, Mr Proudfoot's cheeks started rippling, making his face look like a storm-tossed ocean. "This is daylight robbery!" he thundered. "You can't seriously expect these fine, upstanding people to accept this paltry sum. It's totally and utterly unacceptable."

"Fine," growled Lady Grubnot, "take these snivelling salmonella-spreading failures to another crisp manufacturer and see how far you get with them! Your understanding of the business world is woefully naïve, Mr Proudfoot. We are talking here about a company whose output has been associated with one of the deadliest bacterium known to humans. People eating the Petrucis' crisps could easily start dropping down dead in the next few weeks. I am used to dealing with successful entrepreneurs not third-rate consumer-killers."

"We are not third-rate or killers," said Sonia. "We've made a big success of our company. This just seems like a case of very, very bad luck. We're sure that the leak happened just hours before Mr Proudfoot inspected it."

"I don't care *when* it happened! Why would I or any other reasonable business person pay market rates on a set-up as risky as yours? The sum you are asking is ludicrous. My adjusted figure is far more realistic. So wake up and smell the foul aroma of salt and vinegar, or whatever beastly flavourings you use!"

The Petrucis, who hadn't seen Lady Grubnot's sums, looked as if they had both just been hit in the solar plexus.

"I'm begging you to reconsider," said Proudfoot, clearly trying to keep his temper. "The Petrucis are facing a hideous challenge and the outcome of this meeting will have very powerful consequences for the rest of their lives. I beseech you to show some compassion."

Lady Grubnot stared icily at Proudfoot, her bones highlighted in the half-light, giving her a half-skeleton, half-human visage. "I am a business-woman, Mr Proudfoot, not a philanthropist or a lifestyle coach. I don't do compassion. I suggest they accept my terms and sign on the dotted line right now or I'll throw all three of you off my island!"

Proudfoot was so incensed, he thumped his right fist into the palm of his left hand, like a toddler about to have a full-blown tantrum.

"I need to speak to the Petrucis in private for a few minutes," he announced, huffing and shaking his head angrily. He motioned for Michael and Sonia to stand up and accompany him to one of the far corners of the room. There they stood in a hud-dle, whispering feverishly to each other, while Lady Grubnot eyed them with a spiteful gaze.

What are they going to do? thought Emily. *Sign away their livelihoods to this despicable dictator or try to find another buyer. I'd stay a million miles away from her.*

But it wasn't just the Petrucis Emily felt sorry for. Mr Proudfoot was clearly distressed too. He was putting up such a strong battle for the Petrucis and

Emily willed him on. *Don't accept her terms. Keep your dignity and leave right now!*

After ten minutes of arguments and counterarguments the three finally walked back to face Lady Grubnot.

"With a very heavy heart we are going to accept your offer," said Mr Proudfoot, trying to look calm and in control while inside he clearly felt as if he'd just been crushed beneath the wheels of a ten-ton truck.

Wrong move, thought Emily. *Come on, Mr Proudfoot. Don't let the Petrucis agree to this!*

"We think it's better to get something rather than nothing," said Michael.

"Excellent decision," said Lady Grubnot, producing a pre-prepared contract. She handed it over to the Petrucis.

Emily's eyebrows raised in suspicion. Lady Grubnot was clearly ready for this situation.

"We'll need to show it to our solicitor before we sign it," said Sonia.

"I'm afraid it's a time-limited offer," stated Lady Grubnot. "The time is this second. The limit is now."

The shell-shocked Petrucis looked at each other in despair. They turned to face Proudfoot.

"I'm afraid," said Proudfoot, "that in the circumstances this is almost certainly going to be the only offer you'll get. With a heavy heart and much regret I would advise you to take it." He glowered at Lady Grubnot. She pulled a sickly sweet smile back at him.

"Sign here, here and here," said Lady Grubnot, handing them a pen.

In a mesmerised silence the Petrucis scrawled their names on the document. Lady Grubnot snatched it back from them and clutched it to her chest protectively. She then pulled down a steel tin from a shelf, carefully counted out a meagre pile of notes and handed them over.

"Would you two please go down to the boat and wait for me there," said Proudfoot to the Pwetrucis, raising himself to his full height and seeming to get a second wind. "I would like to have a quiet word with Lady Grubnot alone."

He spat out her name as if it were some rarely uttered obscenity.

The Petrucis nodded their thanks to him, shuffled out and shut the door behind them, broken people. They left the building and started making their way back to the south jetty.

Emily watched in fascination as Lady Grubnot and Mr Proudfoot stood facing each other like two warriors on an open plain.

Lay into her, Mr Proudfoot, willed Emily. *Scream and shout at her; tell her how despicable she is. Let her have the full thing: fireworks masked as words, explosions disguised as sentences!*

The only sound in the great hall was the crackling of the fire and the wind outside, as Emily gazed at these two sparring partners.

They eyed each other furiously for a few more seconds.

Emily had had enough.

She didn't want to see any more of this verbal battle. She knew the score. The poor Petrucis had fallen on hard times and, in spite of Mr Proudfoot's best efforts, Lady Grubnot had bought them out and stitched them up. It was horrid.

She scampered from the breakfast room, out of the kitchen window and back towards the shack, sensing that Lady Grubnot's power, wealth and greed were growing by the second.

Chapter Seventeen
A Crucial Piece of Paper

Friday was the day of the third subversive act. Lady Grubnot was in a fouler mood than ever. Her joy at ruining the Petrucis had clearly faded quickly. She stomped about the production room, muttering to herself about a strange unexplained pain in her neck and whether or not she should have a hearing test. She was spoiling for a fight, for someone to berate, to lacerate someone with her vindictive temper. It was only an hour into the working day when she grabbed Emily's elbow.

"Were you just talking to that other little sewer rat?" she demanded.

"If you mean Paul," Emily replied quietly, not looking directly at Lady Grubnot but a short distance over the Lady's left shoulder, "then no I wasn't."

Lady Grubnot moved a pace to the left so that Emily was now looking directly at her.

"Speak up!" cried Lady Grubnot, her face twisting with anger.

"I wasn't talking to him, I just nodded at him." Emily switched her gaze and now directed it just beyond Lady Grubnot's *right* shoulder.

"STOP MOVING YOUR EYES!" hissed Lady Grubnot, moving to the right.

"I'm not moving them," replied Emily, looking to the left of the Lady again. "You're moving your body."

Emily would have liked to laugh but she knew that this wasn't an option.

"I've got my eye on you, you disgusting vermin-like child!" gasped Lady Grubnot, moving to the left again.

"I understand," replied Emily, switching her eyes back to Lady Grubnot's right. "I'll be extra careful to say nothing to him at all times."

Lady Grubnot's entire face started twitching as she moved to the right. Emily nodded politely and started moving away.

"Left, right, right, left!" snarled Lady Grubnot to herself, feeling dizzy and disorientated. "First my ears, then my neck, now my eyes. Is there something wrong with me? Maybe I have a condition. Maybe I'm going slightly mad."

Emily heard all of these anxious words but she carried on walking.

As dusk was beginning to settle, Emily and Paul were on their way back from picking some berries when they came across Clemence. He was wearing his brown gardener's jumper and grey horticultural trousers while standing on a small stepladder and snipping a hedge with some large shears.

"Greetings." He beamed at them. "I'm glad I've seen you."

He climbed down from the ladder, grabbed some chopped leaves and stuffed them into a black refuse sack. "I'm so sorry I had to rush off the other day. In spite of my efforts, my souffle got burnt and Lady Grubnot was none too pleased."

"Sorry about that," said Emily.

Clemence stood there for a moment, scratching his cheek. "I tell you what," he said. "As a way of saying thank you for fixing my stilts, would you two like to take a look at my inventing room?"

"Yes please!" cried Paul.

"Surely Lady Grubnot will go mad if she finds us in the manor house," said Emily.

"If we're quiet she won't know." Clemence grinned. "She never visits the fourth floor, but we'll avoid the main entrance, just to be on the safe side."

And so it came to pass that after climbing a long, twisting fire escape at the back of the manor house, Emily and Paul found themselves in a large rectangular attic room, containing two desks, a large black workbench and several ladders of differing sizes. A big pane of glass in the ceiling let natural light flow inside. Every work surface and centimetre of floor space was covered with the tools of the inventor's trade: cables, wires, spanners, screwdrivers, rulers, test tubes, hammers, drills, half-eaten sandwiches and a thousand other things. It was as if Clemence had opened a dust-covered toolbox when he moved in and emptied its contents in a haphazard fashion.

"Wow!" muttered Emily. "This place is amazing."

"I'm very fond of it." Clemence smiled, easing down into a tattered brown swivel chair. "If I didn't have to perform a multitude of duties for Lady Grubnot, I could quite happily spend all of my time up here."

"Are you working on anything else – apart from the stilts and your pay distribution unit?" asked Emily. She would have mentioned the wearable ear alerters but she'd only found out about those when she'd been hiding by the fence and she didn't want to explain this to Clemence.

"You really want to know my current plans?" enquired Clemence, his eyes lighting up, astonished that anyone was actually taking an interest in his creations. After all, listening to Lady Grubnot's fierce attacks on all he created was a trifle dispiriting.

"Definitely!" Emily and Paul nodded enthusiastically.

Clemence leant over to a large wooden chest on the floor, propped open the lid and started pulling things out at an alarming pace. "Let me see… This week is the stilts, the pay distribution unit and the ear alerters. Next week is the robot grass cutter and the self-inflating banana balloon, the week after that is the radio socks and the super-action bread maker that doesn't make bread. All of these of course are soon-to-be-patented."

"Why is it called a bread maker when it doesn't make bread?" asked Emily.

"It makes crackers," replied Clemence.

"So why didn't you call it a cracker –"

Emily nudged Paul in the ribs and he stopped talking.

"Sorry to interrupt you," said Emily, who was intoxicated by the room and all of its fascinating inventions and equipment, "but is there a toilet up here?" She had suddenly become aware that a great opportunity had presented itself. This was her first time outside the manor house kitchen. This was a chance to carry out some surveillance work, just like Pirate Summers did when he first entered the Cave of Ill Fortune.

"Of course." Clemence nodded. "It's down the corridor and is the only other room on this floor. You can't miss it. Now I'm going to find my soon-to-be-patented talking egg cover. I think you'll both like it." He began rummaging around in the wooden chest.

"Back in a minute," said Emily, winking at Paul and stepping out of the room into the light yellow-tiled corridor.

She walked forward briskly, passed the toilet and spotted a narrow staircase up ahead. Looking behind to make sure Clemence hadn't followed her, she hurried down these stairs and found herself in another corridor, this one's floor covered with a wilting beige carpet.

She tried the first door she came across. It was some sort of storeroom, with pots of paint stacked on top of each other. The second led to a cleaning cupboard, replete with mops, buckets and cleaning fluids. The third door led to somewhere far more interesting.

It was a room with two large chandeliers, blue wallpaper, purple drapes, a rather old red chaise longue, a tatty green sofa in need of repair and a vast mahogany writing table. Although the room was shabby, it felt important. There were grey files lined up on shelves, and box files marked "Business Correspondence". The air smelled musty, of old cracked leather furniture and slightly damp walls. It looked like Lady Grubnot's office, her inner sanctum. Was this the nerve centre of her entire operation? Could the facts and figures about her company be stored in this room?

At the prospect of this, Emily's heartbeat accelerated like a motorcycle thief speeding away from the forces of law and order, but she didn't turn back. There might be something in here that could help build on her psychological war. Maybe some nugget of information lay in this room, something that could somehow, in some way, be used against Lady Grubnot?

Emily knew that if Lady Grubnot found her in here there would be trouble like no trouble before, but she pushed this thought aside and hurried over to the table. On it were three piles of paperwork. She flicked through these. They were bills, invoices and delivery dockets. Next to them were two grey files. These contained information about delivery of the crisps, the routes her drivers took, their destinations. The last item on the desk was a ring-bound grey notebook. Under barely legible headings like "Royal Cousins" and "Royal Family Gatherings" were lines and lines of indecipherable, squiggly handwriting that Emily recognised as that of Lady Grubnot's.

Crouching down, Emily pulled open the top drawer of three. Inside were paperclips, pencils, sharpeners and other odds and ends of stationary. The middle drawer contained a small paper folder. Inside this were letters to and from her various suppliers: the farmer who grew the Medlock potatoes, the company that made her foil packets. There were also a couple to Mr Faraday.

The bottom drawer was empty. Emily felt disappointment moving in on her in pincer-like movements. What a complete waste of time! She'd come in here at great personal risk to find out…nothing. She banged her fist on the table and as she did so a tiny strip of white suddenly appeared in the bottom drawer. It was the top of a piece of paper. She reached in and tried to pull it out. It was wedged under a thin shelf of wood. It was a concealed compartment!

After tugging and twisting for a minute, Emily finally managed to pull up the thin wooden slice and take out the paper.

It read:

HIGH-END CRISP COMPETITORS – SIX MONTH REVIEW

TEMPUS MARKET SNACKFOODS – Closed due to gutting by fire
ABLE VALLEY CRISP CO. – Closed due to infestation of rats
SHERAM COUNTY SNACK COMPANY – Closed due to severe flooding

THE HILL TREE CRISP CONSORTIUM –
Closed due to boiler explosion
PETRUCIS CRISPS – Closed due to salmo-
nella in production process
RIDGE FARM CRISPS – ?

Emily stared at the list for a few moments, letting the
words dig and dive their way into her brain. By the
look of this paper, five of Lady Grubnot's crisp company rivals had been put out of business in the last
six months, and Emily recognised the name of the
second last one. Petrucis. That had been the name
of the couple that she'd spied on in the great hall –
the ones that Mr Proudfoot had tried to save.

But what was this on the other side of the paper?
A list of sums paid to one…Arthur Proudfoot. For
"Services Delivered". Why on earth would she be
paying him? It made no sense. They'd looked like
they'd have been happy to kill each other.

And then a terrible thought hit Emily and she
straightened up as if a coat hanger had suddenly
been inserted into the top half of her body. No.
Surely not. It couldn't be possible. Could it? Emily
shuddered as if Lady Grubnot had just entered the
room and were glaring at her with repulsion in their
eyes. The walls seemed to be closing in on her, the
purple curtains were going to ensnare her, the writing desk would grow tentacles to wrap her up.

She shook her head and focused on her question. And her question was this. What if it had all
been an act? What if Mr Proudfoot was actually in
league with the Lady? He'd said he was from some

crisp industry organisation and that he'd inspected the Petrucis' factory and found salmonella. Was it possible that he'd *planted* the salmonella there? That would be utterly, stupendously evil. It would mean that he and Lady Grubnot had together ruined the Petrucis' business and by the look of it their lives.

Emily tried to assimilate all of these thoughts but the more she pieced things together the more she was sure she'd hit on the truth. There could be no other reason for Lady Grubnot paying Arthur Proudfoot. He was a charlatan; a master of the foulest kind of sham.

If this was the case, then could they be behind the catastrophes that had struck down her other competitors too? Fires, rats, flooding and explosions. Of course they could! It was outlandish. It was horrendous. It was genius! By sabotaging those other companies and then buying them out, Lady Grubnot would have the ENTIRE posh crisp market to herself. And if that happened, surely there would be even greater demand for Grubnot's Exclusives? Would Lady Grubnot then increase her output, making her workers toil even harder? What an awful prospect.

And then Emily recalled the empty box she and Paul had spotted in the pantry with the label: BERKSHIRE CRISPS. That name wasn't on this list. Maybe they weren't a competitor? Maybe they were a non-posh crisp company? Maybe, as Paul had suggested, Clemence had covertly ordered some for himself?

Her thoughts switched to Ridge Farm Crisps, the last name on the list. There was a question mark

112

beside them. There was no mention of their closing down. That must mean Lady Grubnot hadn't got to them...yet.

Emily was still staring at the list and thinking hard when she heard her name being called.

It was Clemence.

Quickly, she flung the piece of paper back in the drawer, fitted the wooden shelf on top of it, slammed the drawer shut and raced out of the room. She sped back up the stairs and found Clemence knocking on the toilet door and calling her name. Paul was standing beside him, looking anxious.

"Sorry," panted Emily, reaching the top of the stairs, "I got a bit lost on my way back."

"No problem, but I need to clean out the fireplace in the great hall so I'd best be off to find my chimney-sweep outfit. It's been a great pleasure showing you my humble inventing space and I'm grateful for your interest in my work. It's not fully appreciated in...other spheres."

Emily smiled. "We think it's brilliant...and we think you're exceedingly clever!"

Clemence blushed and gave Emily and Paul a bow.

"You're welcome to visit again," said Clemence. "I've only shown you a tiny selection of my output."

"Thanks," said Paul. "We'd love to come again."

"I suggest you take the fire escape out for reasons I previously stated."

Emily and Paul walked towards the fire escape while Clemence strode off in the opposite direction. Emily ushered Paul in front of her and he opened the fire door.

"Oh, there is one other thing," she said, as Paul walked outside.

"Yes?" asked Clemence, coming to a halt and looking round.

"I heard Lady Grubnot on the phone the other day saying something about lots of other crisp companies shutting down because of accidents and mishaps. Is that true?"

"Indeed it is," Clemence said gravely. "I believe Lady Grubnot has bought all of their stock and machinery for a bargain – she told me this in a whir of excitement. They exist no more."

"That's what I thought," replied Emily. "Thank you." She was now totally convinced that she was right about Lady Grubnot's scheme. Infiltrate the other companies, get them closed down and then buy all of their resources for a pittance. And Ridge Farm, the last of her competitors, would in all likelihood be expecting a surprise visit from Mr Proudfoot, if it was indeed he who carried out the dirty, crisp-destroying missions. Why, he could even be on his way to Ridge Farm right now.

Clemence nodded and carried on along the landing. Emily joined Paul on the fire escape for the climb down.

CHAPTER EIGHTEEN
A NEW DIRECTION
FOR EMILY

Before they'd reached the shack, a plan had formed in Emily's mind. The second that supper was over, she hurried outside and got to work. At the back of the shack, she moved all of her mum's herb pots out of the way and pushed a low wooden bench against the shack wall. Paul came out after a while to see what she was up to.

"Can you pass me that piece of rope please?" she asked. Emily was kneeling over a collection of large leaves, branches and rusty metal parts from a broken wheelbarrow.

"What are you doing?" he asked, handing her the length of rope. She used it to lash two branches together.

"I'm making a tent."

"A tent? What for? We've already got a place to sleep."

"I think it would be fun to do a little bit of camping."

"Camping! What, like Pirate Summers on Skull-Crossed Cove? That's a brilliant idea! Can I come?"

Emily looked up at Paul. He was right. That was exactly where she'd got the idea. But it was a solo mission. "Not this time," she replied, "but soon, I promise you." She reached for some leaves and carefully slid them through a hole between two lengths of metal.

Paul's bottom lip dropped and for a second she thought he was going to cry, but he scowled instead.

"What's going on out here?" asked Janet. She and Monty had stepped outside to enjoy some cool night air.

"Emily's making a tent," huffed Paul.

"I'm going on a camping trip after work tomorrow," said Emily, "by myself."

"Really?" Janet frowned.

"And miss one of my meals?" asked Monty. "Are you mad?"

"Where will you camp?" asked Janet, frowning deeper when she spied her herb pots all piled up together in a corner.

"Somewhere on the east side of the island."

"You'll stick to the paths won't you?" said Monty.

"Yes, Father," sighed Emily. "My tent and I will stay well within the boundaries of safety."

"She says I can go with her next time," said Paul in a more positive tone.

"Won't you freeze, sleeping in a structure covered by leaves?" asked Janet. "I mean, the nights are pretty cold at the minute. Come on, Emily. Go camping when it's a bit warmer. I'll brew you up a double delicious hot tea tomorrow night."

"I'll wear two jumpers," said Emily. "Now if you don't mind I have loads to do."

"She's strong-willed," observed her father with a shrug of his shoulders.

"OK, it's fine I suppose," said Janet. "But don't stay up too late tonight. It's unfortunately a work day tomorrow."

"As if I could forget," groaned Emily, her triangular tent structure slowly starting to take shape.

Emily did stay up late. She finished the tent some time after all of the others had retired for the night. But that wasn't all. Tiptoeing indoors, she grabbed a candle, a piece of paper and a pencil and stepped back outside. Lighting the candle, she leant against the shack wall and wrote a message headed "ZAK". This she placed into a small bottle from the kitchen.

Then, holding the candle aloft with one hand and clutching the bottle in the other, she hurried eastwards towards her and Zak's meeting point. It was spooky heading out there in the dark. Shadows spiralled and flowed in the candlelight, reminding her of the shadowy Sand People that attacked Pirate Summers in *The Walk of the Night Folk*.

Brushing the now familiar bushes aside she walked up to the fence and pushed the bottle through the hole, making sure she touched no section of the wooden fence. It landed on the other side with a thud.

Hurrying back, she hoped that the wind wouldn't carry it off or a ravenous seagull wouldn't try to eat it as a meal. It had to be there on the ground for Zak to see when he arrived tomorrow. The note contained the stages of the new phase in Emily's campaign. Yes, she was pleased with her anti-Lady-Grubnot subversions, but this new project was very different. It was far, far bigger, just like Zak had said it would need to be. This could be massive. This felt like the possible start of a proper fightback.

CHAPTER NINETEEN
CONCEALED

"Have you got your pyjamas?" asked Janet.

"Yes."

"And your toothbrush?" asked Monty.

"Yes."

"Leave the poor girl alone," laughed Bob, placing an arm round his granddaughter's shoulders as they all stood at the front of the shack. The working day had just finished and everyone was keen to get out of their work clothes, but not before they'd bidden Emily farewell. The sun hadn't set yet and the ground was still warm. A nearby stream bubbled gently.

"She's a fine, independent kid and I think this camping trip will be good for her: a night in the outdoors; a meeting with nature. I say grab a bit of freedom. The best of luck to you, young lady."

"Thanks, Granddad."

Emily had her tent slung over one shoulder, and a small bag of necessities clutched in her right hand. She was in a hurry.

"Don't forget I'm coming next time," Paul reminded her.

She'd managed to grab Paul for a few seconds here and there during the day to explain the bare bones of what she was going to attempt and to outline his vital role in this caper. He was thrilled and excited to be involved, and had promised he wouldn't mention a word to anyone. She hadn't told him about Zak because she thought he might be jealous that someone else was helping her, but she was determined to introduce the two of them in the near future...if she was still alive in that time frame.

"If any of the adults discover a scintilla of information about this undertaking, all of my plans will be in tatters," she'd warned him.

"I'm off then," said Emily. Her parents and Granddad gave her pecks on the cheek and waved her off. Paul said he needed to go and collect some stones and he dashed away on his own.

Emily acted ultra-quickly. Timing was going to be everything in the next ten minutes. She reached the stretch of path where she'd be camping and dumped her tent and bag on the floor. Then she retraced her steps and took the path leading up to the production room.

"Over here," called Paul. His head was jutting out round the side of the building and he was beckoning to her. She joined him and they slunk forward until they reached the window Lady Grubnot had broken when she'd flung Clemence's soon-to-be-patented pay distribution unit at him.

Clemence hadn't had time to repair it, so Paul had pulled the remaining pieces of glass out and stuck some tape round the edges of the window frame as

Emily had instructed. She nodded admiringly at his handiwork and a minute later they were both inside.

It felt strange being in the production room when all the lights were off and none of the other workers were around, a bit like the time between sleeping and waking up, when the world slowly appears to you, frame by frame. They crept across the lino towards the forklift in the loading bay. In the dim light its silhouette made it look like some giant metal sculpture, its powers dormant. The fork-lift's blades were carrying piles of boxes stamped with GRUBNOT'S EXCLUSIVE CRISPS – boxes that Emily and the others had only finished stacking a short while ago. Paul grabbed a ladder and held it steady while Emily shinned up it and began unload-ing the boxes from one of the piles next to the cab. She passed these down to Paul, who stacked them against a wall. He then hurried off and returned a few seconds later with an empty box he'd nabbed from the storeroom.

"Are you totally sure about this?" he asked, the full drama of the situation really dawning on him. "Are you one hundred per cent certain that Lady Grubnot's been shutting down all of her rivals and that she's definitely going to try to close down the last of them? It's pretty important. You're putting yourself at huge risk for this."

Emily nodded. "I'm as sure as I can be, and I have to at least try to stop this part of her plan. Someone's got to. Now come on!"

❧ ❧ ❧

They finished a few seconds before Clemence arrived. He strode in and unlocked the double doors of the loading bay, opening them as far as they would go. He then climbed into the forklift driver's seat.

"She wants croque-monsieur for dinner tonight," he was muttering to himself. "I'm not sure what the croque is and I have no idea who the monsieur may be. Hopefully my small but carefully selected collection of cookery books will place me on the correct culinary path. Anything will be easier than eggs Benedict."

Having finished this mini conversation with himself, Clemence turned the ignition and the forklift moved forward and out through the loading-bay doors. The path down to the south jetty was pockmarked with holes so the ride was somewhat bumpy. Apart from the odd jolt the journey was uneventful; at least for him.

At the south jetty, Clemence stopped, disembarked, unlocked a giant gate in the fence and drove through. Mr Faraday and Zak were there waiting for him. When Clemence brought the forklift to a final halt, the three of them began loading the boxes onto the boat. Zak made sure it was he who lifted the bottom box of the back left-hand pile as Emily had instructed. He placed this carefully on board, right where he could keep an eye on it.

"OK," said Mr Faraday, when all of the boxes were on board. "Let's give you all of your potatoes and your week's shopping, Mr Clemence, and then we'll be off."

It took a further few minutes to unload the provisions onto the blades of the forklift. Following this, they said their goodbyes, and as Clemence steered the forklift back up to the loading bay, having closed the large gate behind him, Mr Faraday's boat set off for Northurst Harbour.

The box that Zak had been so determined to handle himself did not contain crisps.

It contained Emily Cruet.

Back at the loading bay she had climbed into the empty box Paul had grabbed (in which they'd made some tiny holes for breathing purposes), squeezed herself down and waited while Paul taped it up. He'd then placed the box on the bottom left corner of the blades, and restacked all of the other offloaded boxes on top of her one. So she was there, inside a cardboard box, pretending to be a large mound of crisp packets.

And it meant that, for the first time in her entire life, Emily Cruet was leaving Grubnot Island.

CHAPTER TWENTY
DELIVERY AT NORTHURST

The boat ride to Northurst Harbour took fifteen minutes. Although cramped, the journey wasn't too uncomfortable for Emily. She presumed this was because her mind was so focused on visiting the mainland, even if it was only for what she hoped would be a shortish visit. Mr Faraday moored at bay three, Northurst Harbour, and he and Zak started unloading the boxes and handing them over to the waiting lorry drivers, Zak keeping a constant eye on Emily's box.

But when one of the drivers spoke to him he lost sight of it for a few seconds. When he looked round he was horrified to spot Mr Faraday going for that very box. It was a calamity! As soon as Mr Faraday felt its weight, the game would be up.

"Mr Faraday!" he shouted, running over to him.

Mr Faraday was crouching down on the boat, his hands millimetres away from the box. "Yes?" he asked, freezing for a moment.

"I think Barry's a box down. You'd better go and check it out."

Barry was one of the drivers. He wasn't missing a box but it was the only way Zak could think of to remove Mr Faraday from the crucial spot.

Mr Faraday sighed, stood up, and strode off to talk to Barry.

Zak leapt onto the boat and picked up the Emily box. Attempting to make it look like he was merely carrying a box stuffed with crisp packets, he made for the area between two of the vans. Placing it on the floor, he tore off the tape. Emily jumped out and scuttled over to hide behind a tree, dragging the empty box with her. Zak walked back out, whistling to himself, and went to unload the last of the boxes.

"Barry isn't missing a box," said Mr Faraday. "You must have made a mistake."

"Stupid me," said Zak. "Sorry about that."

"Stick those last ones in Jeff's lorry and then you're done for the day," Mr Faraday said, handing Zak a couple of banknotes.

"Cheers," said Zak, pocketing the cash and finishing his last delivery.

"Right," called Mr Faraday, "all boxes loaded; all vehicles ready. Off you go, lads."

The crisp-bearing lorries revved their meaty engines and the drivers pulled away from Northurst Harbour, some going left, some going right.

"See you next week," said Mr Faraday, locking the boat before walking off to get his car.

Zak waited until Mr Faraday had driven off and then he ran over to the tree. Emily popped her head out.

"Welcome to the world," said Zak with a grin.

CHAPTER TWENTY-ONE
A BRAND NEW WORLD
(NOT FORGETTING CAGS)

From the second Emily climbed out of the box, she stared at her surroundings with saucer-sized eyes and an open mouth. There was a fish-and-chip shop with its vinegary aroma and queue of good-humoured people, their faces illuminated by the flashing neon sign. Here was a young child, sitting beside its mother on a low brick wall, gobbling a red-and-white ball that balanced on top of a brown chequered cylinder. A bit further up the road a group of lads were kicking a ball around on a small patch of grass, wearing different hooded garments and peaked caps while laughing and joking with each other. Each sight, sound and smell seemed to be pulling Emily into a vast new dimension, the shackles of her tiny, imprisoned life snapping one by one. It was as if she'd been living in a world smothered in grey and had suddenly stepped out into a kingdom of colours – bright and bold.

"This is amazing!" she mouthed in delight.

Zak followed her gaze and shrugged his shoulders. "You get used to it when you've been here for eleven years," he said. "Now what was the name of that crisp place you told me?"

"It's called Ridge Farm Crisps," said Emily. "I presume we need a big fold-out map to find it."

"Don't worry about the folding-out bit, but a map, yes. My phone's low on juice. Good for a call but not so good for surfing. Follow me."

Zak hurried across the road. Emily waited a few seconds. She had no idea what Zak was talking about and, anyway, she had so much to study. Everything, every tiny detail, was completely new to her: the pavements, the bus stop with its garish posters, the telephone wires stretching from house to house, the brown puppy being held on a tight leash by an elderly man with a handlebar moustache. She stared at a young couple arguing, the man with a short beard, the woman with a yellow beret. Finally she started crossing the road to join Zak.

"Move!" Zak shouted as an orange double-decked vehicle came speeding round the corner and made a beeline for Emily. She took Zak's hint and ran to the opposite side sharpish.

"I know all this must be freaking you out," said Zak, "but it's probably best not to stand in the middle of the road admiring your surroundings when a bus is coming your way."

"Of course," said Emily, "it's just that we don't have cars or buses on the island."

Zak smiled. "I understand. What do you think of it so far?"

"I think... I think it's incredible," gushed Emily. "What's that building with the big flashing red sign?"

"It's the Northurst Picture House. It's where they show films – you know those moving picture things I told you about?"

Before Emily could ask another question, Zak took her by the elbow and led her inside a small brown building named JEM'S INTERNET CAFÉ.

The room inside was square in shape, with recently painted mauve walls and ten or so small booths each containing a chair, a desk and a computer. Of course Emily had never seen a computer before, and she was instantly fascinated by them. The space was dimly lit and there was a faint smell of some sort of cheese in the air. Zak handed over some money to a scrawny young man who was reading a comic, presumably Jem, as he had a huge tattoo of the word "Jem" on the side of his neck. "Station ten," said Jem, without looking up.

"This way," said Zak, guiding her to an empty booth marked "10". He sat down, grabbed a small object on the right of the desk and used it to move an arrow around the screen. He interspersed these manoeuvres with hitting numbers and letters on a flat black panel in front of the screen.

"What is *it*?" asked Emily, pointing at the machine.

"It's a computer," replied Zak. "There are millions, probably billions of them in the world. They're good and they're bad."

"What are you doing with those letters and numbers?"

"Just give me a minute," said Zak. "It was Ridge Farm Crisps wasn't it?"

Emily nodded.

Zak hit some more keys and a few seconds later a message came up on the screen:

RIDGE FARM CRISPS
RIDGE FARM
OTTER WAY
NETTISHAM
NN7 9UU

"How did you do that?" marvelled Emily.

"It's called the internet," replied Zak. "When you're really free I'll teach you how to use it."

When you're really free. Emily's heart pulsed as she thought of everyone back on Grubnot Island and the seriousness of her mission. Finding out the location of Ridge Farm Crisps was a great first achievement. But there was so much more to do after that. Was she capable of pulling any of this off? It all suddenly felt horribly daunting and a tiny part of her thought about making a dash back to the island. *No way,* she told herself. *Not when you've just arrived on the mainland.*

A map came up on the screen, showing Northurst Harbour, Ridge Farm and the distance between them.

"It's thirty-six miles," said Zak.

"Are we walking?" asked Emily.

"No chance," laughed Zak, tapping a few more keys. There was a whirring sound and a piece of paper came out of another black machine with the map printed on its surface.

Emily gaped at these wondrous pieces of technology. She'd love to take them apart and discover the mechanisms that made them work; maybe not today though.

"And you said in that note that you think she and this Proudfoot guy have been deliberately infiltrating her rivals and shutting them down?"

Emily nodded.

Zak typed some more and a page appeared on the screen listing all of the country's high-end crisp companies. It had all six of the companies Emily had seen in Lady Grubnot's notebook plus Grubnot's Exclusives. Beside five of them were press reports and information about the cessation of their businesses.

"She's really going for it, isn't she?" murmured Zak. "I think you're right, Emily. She wants to be the only company left in that part of the market. The top dog."

Emily looked confused.

"It means the boss."

"And she's the kind of person who always gets what she wants," noted Emily.

"We'll see about that," said Zak, standing up and walking back over to the scrawny guy. "Excuse me, mate, can I borrow your phone to send a text message? Mine's got no power."

The guy looked at Zak as if he were a dung beetle on a particularly stinky grub crawl. "Just one," he said, reaching into his jacket pocket.

Emily had seen Lady Grubnot speaking on a mobile phone a couple of times but the Lady had

never done any of the furious finger-tapping that Zak
did when Jem reluctantly handed him his mobile.

When he'd finished his mad finger dance, he
held onto the phone for a few moments until it
made a whooshing noise. He studied something on
its screen, passed the phone back to Jem, and then
led Emily outside.

He grinned. "Brilliant. She's on her way."

Emily didn't get a chance to ask who "she" was
because she was still drinking in all of the details of
the mainland a few minutes later when a battered
white car with two orange stripes down each side
and a pockmarked yellow rear spoiler hurtled round
the corner and pulled up with a screech outside
the internet café. The car's front number plate was
hanging by a thread, its back bumper was missing
and the tyres looked like their rubber surfaces were
just about clinging on. Stuck to the roof was a handmade cardboard sign with the word TAXI scrawled
in shaky blue writing.

The driver was a girl who looked no more than
a couple of years older than Emily and Zak. She had
short, blonde hair, a tiny red nose ring, very small
ears, eyebrows that looked like carefully twisted gui-
tar strings and deep amber eyes resembling those of
an ancient Egyptian goddess.

"Thanks, Cags," said Zak, climbing into the front
passenger seat, while motioning for Emily to get in
the back. "Emily, meet Cags, Cags, meet Emily."

When Emily was inside, Zak turned round and
showed her how to buckle the seat belt. Then he
studied the map he'd printed out. "Right," he said

after a minute, "head for Ogden Way. And take it easy. This is Emily's first time in a car."

"There's a first time for everything," said Cags, ignoring Zak's request for mellow driving and slamming her foot down on the accelerator pedal. The car leapt along the street. Emily flew forward but her seat belt pulled her back.

Cags yanked the wheel down hard left and the car veered round a corner.

"Zak here says you've been having a bit of trouble out on Grubnot Island," said Cags, swerving past a shopping trolley someone had left at the side of the road.

Looking guilty, Zak said, "I've only told her the basics and I haven't said anything to anyone else, I promise, Emily. She's my cousin and totally trustworthy. Well, sort of."

"Hey!" cried Cags, punching Zak in the ribs.

"That's fine," Emily replied. "It's really kind of you to come and pick us up."

"Business has been quiet tonight," said Cags. "So it's good to give this beast a bit of a runaround."

By "beast" Emily assumed Cags was referring to the vehicle they were in. "Is this car yours?" she asked, holding onto a small handle above her door, fearing that her life was possibly about to end thirty miles short of Ridge Farm.

"Nah," said Cags, leaning her right elbow on the open window. "It belongs to my older brother, Bez. It isn't a real taxi. I just like to borrow it when the mood takes me and earn a bit of extra cash. The taxi sign is pretty cool though, isn't it? There's nothing like a homemade sign for attracting customers."

Emily nodded. "Yes, it looks very professional." She watched as the houses and shops of Northurst faded behind them and the car started cruising down a wide country lane with hedgerows and buttercups on either side.

Cags beamed with pride and overtook a smaller car with an incredible burst of speed. "Zak says these are crisp makers you're going to visit," she said. "Why do you need to see them? Can't get enough of the crunchy circles?"

"They might be facing a serious problem," replied Emily. "I think someone is going to try to shut them down."

"What, like industrial sabotage?" said Cags, her eyes going wild with intrigue. "Sounds like one of those Sunday night TV shows my dad likes."

"Something like that," said Zak, "but it's all a big secret at the minute."

"Know what you're saying," replied Cags, touching her nose ring. "Keep it in the family."

Emily looked puzzled at this turn of phrase.

"She means she won't tell anyone," explained Zak.

Ten minutes later, Zak told Cags to turn left onto a steep hill and then a sharp right. Cags flicked the steering wheel this way and that as though she were swatting a fly, nearly sending them hurtling over the edge of the road.

Emily noticed there was quite a sharp drop into a valley beyond the edge of the road and decided she'd be more than happy not to make the valley's acquaintance. But in spite of the fact that Cag's driving was utterly and totally mad, as well as scaring Emily, it also excited her. It made her feel alive in a way she had never really felt before.

And somehow, as Cags sped round corners and hurtled down slopes, she managed to keep the car on the right track. After a good few miles swerving from side to side on a particularly windy road, they hit a long stretch of flat tarmac and stayed on this for about fifteen minutes.

"Take the next right," said Zak, holding up the map. "It's the track that leads up to Ridge Farm."

When Cags took this corner they hit a bumpy, rutted track and the car momentarily left the tarmac.

"Nice one!" Cags grinned when the vehicle hit the road again. "That'll toughen up this beast's suspension!"

"Or break it," muttered Zak.

On went the "taxi". Thorny bushes grew on one side of the track and a row of willowy saplings stood on the other. Now that they were nearly there, questions started nipping up to bite Emily's brain like a bunch of yappy dogs. What if the Ridge Farm people didn't believe her story? Might they call her an intruder and throw her off their land? Would they phone Lady Grubnot and say an escaped worker from her island was spreading poisonous rumours about her? And what if Emily got stuck here on the mainland – what if she never saw her parents again?

Her thoughts were interrupted by Zak's voice. "OK, pull up here."

Cags thumped the brakes and the car ground to a crunching halt. Up ahead was a barred metal gate with a large sign stating in big black letters: WELCOME TO RIDGE FARM – HOME OF RIDGE FARM CRISPS.

"You do the honours," instructed Cags.

Zak climbed out and walked over to the gate. He tried to pull it open but spotted a locked padlock. He shook his head and climbed back in the car. Before anyone could speak about what they should do next, Cag's phone started ringing, or rather, roaring, like a violent monster, as "Death Beast Bark" was her current ringtone.

She listened for a few seconds and then said, "Come on, Bez. You can do without it for one measly night, can't you?"

She listened to the reply. "Yes, he's with me," she said.

Another pause. "Be reasonable, Bez, I'm on an important mission and I'll split all of my taxi takings with you if you let me have it."

She listened again. "OK, I haven't made any takings tonight but I picked up a few good leads around Northurst Harbour so I won't have any problems picking up some customers. There'll be plenty of money for both of us and –"

But the line must have gone dead, because she pulled a face and slammed the phone down on the dashboard.

"Bez is SO selfish," she sighed. "He wants the car back."

"It is *his* car," pointed out Zak.

"So?" moaned Cags. "He just drives it around with his mates and goes to the chip shop. I run it as a legitimate business. I've got the sign on top and everything."

"And as Emily said, it's a very fine sign," said Zak, "but if Bez wants it back you have to give it him or else he'll never let you use it again."

"He never lets me use it," countered Cags. "I just take it when he's not looking."

"Even more reason to take it back," said Zak.

Cags sighed and turned her head round to face Emily. "I'm really sorry," she said. "I was looking forward to meeting these crisp people. You know, maybe get a few packs. I'm a big, big fan of salty snacks."

"It's fine." Emily smiled. "I didn't expect a ride here so it's been a great bonus. Thank you so much, Cags."

"You drive back and we'll go and see the Ridges," said Zak.

"No can do," replied Cags. "Your mum asked Bez to ask me if you were with me tonight. She said if you're not home pretty sharpish you'll be grounded for a month."

Emily wasn't sure what "grounded" meant – could it mean tied to the ground? That would be a bit of a harsh punishment, especially if you had to stay there for a month. It might even be beyond the repertoire of Lady Grubnot.

The call ended. "What does grounded mean?" asked Emily.

"It means not leave the house for a month," he explained. "Staying in and hearing my mum's awful singing."

"It's OK," said Emily. "Both of you go. I'll do this by myself. That's been the plan all the way along."

"Are you mad?" cried Cags. "There could be vicious guard dogs up ahead who'll rip your head off because they haven't eaten for five seconds."

"Please," said Emily. "It's better this way. This is my problem and if I get into trouble I don't want you two involved."

"I don't like it," said Zak, shaking his head. "We can't just leave you here. How will you get back to Northurst, let alone the island? You heard what Cags said. She won't get the car again tonight."

"I'll work out something," said Emily, whose words sounded far braver than she felt.

"But you have to be back home at a reasonable time tomorrow morning because you've got work," said Zak. "If you're not around everyone will freak out, particularly Lady Grubnot."

"Tomorrow morning is a long time away," said Emily. "I'll get there."

"Well at least take my mobile phone," said Zak. "It's very low on power but it should let you make a call or two, if you're quick. That way you can contact Cags when you're done with the Ridges and she can let me know what's going on."

"Nice one," said Cags. "But just because Bez thinks it's his car and his car alone doesn't mean I can't pick up some passengers on the way home, get some money, split it with him, and take it out again later."

"Forget that," said Zak. "Just keep your phone on so Emily can call you if and when she needs to."

Cags nodded. "No worries."

Zak handed Emily his phone and quickly showed her how to call Cag's number.

"This is great," said Emily, pocketing the phone. She desperately wanted to know exactly how it worked, but that could wait. "Thanks for all of your help." She opened the back door and got out.

"No sweat," said Cags. "Good luck and hopefully see you soon. If there are tons of crisps up there, maybe save a few for me. And if the chips are down, give me a bell."

"Of course." Emily smiled, although she was unsure how a plate of chips and a bell were relevant to her current situation.

"She means keep in touch," said Zak.

Cags grinned. "Phone me."

Emily watched and waved as Cags performed a rapid-fire three-point turn and then headed the beast back down the track. A few seconds later the backlights of the car had vanished from sight.

Telling herself to remain calm now that she was really here at Ridge Farm and it wasn't just an idea in her head, Emily climbed over the metal fence and followed the uneven path round a couple of corners and then right up to an oak-beamed farmhouse. It was a two-storey building with oval windows and great swathes of ivy clinging onto its light brown brickwork. On the roof was an ornate black iron fence

CRISPS

that encircled what looked like a garden overflowing with fascinating-looking plants and small trees. In the distance Emily heard a forlorn cow mooing and a bird cawing somewhere up high, but it was the note taped to the large blue front door that really grabbed her attention.

It carried the day's date and the following message:

**THE RIDGES ARE ON HOLIDAY
FOR TWO WEEKS**

139

CHAPTER TWENTY-TWO
THE RIDGES

Emily looked at the sign and felt her heart plummet like a sandwich dropped from a vast building, the kind of breaded descent that physics teachers tell you can crack a hole in the pavement.

Two weeks!

She couldn't wait two weeks to see the Ridges. By then Mr Proudfoot could have blown up their entire farm and made it look like a freak storm had done it. In two weeks Lady Grubnot could have the entire posh-crisp market all to herself and be making Emily and her co-workers strive twice if not three times as hard. In and out as quick as possible – that had been the plan. Then somehow back to the island and inside her tent with no one – especially not her parents – having even the tiniest clue that she'd visited the mainland.

She'd come all of this way for nothing. She felt like screaming out in rage and disappointment. Then she remembered Zak's phone in her pocket. She dialled Cags's number but just got shouty music and some kind of shrill alarm. Even the gadget was against her.

She slumped down onto the grass verge, her spirits plummeting further at her awful timing. She scolded herself bitterly for lack of planning and foresight. How could she have been so unprepared? Why hadn't she got Zak to do some research to see if the Ridges would be here when she arrived? Plus she had no water or even the smallest scrap of food. In the heady exhilaration of becoming a message-bearing heroine, she'd given almost no thought to the practicalities of her task. Her self-directed fury mixed with the exhaustion of the evening's activities nudged her to curl up in a ball on the grass and fall into a fitful and troubled slumber.

The feel of a wet slobbering tongue on the side of her face woke Emily up.

"Hey, Rufus, stop that!" called a deep male voice.

Emily opened her eyes and found the face of a Golden Labrador right in hers, looking at her and dribbling on her as if she were an interesting new foodstuff. A tall, wiry man with a beard and a woman with her hair in plaits and a soft round face were standing over Emily and looking at her with concern. The man wore a chunky white jumper and faded jeans. The woman sported a multi-coloured dress and a light blue scarf that held up her hair. They both had large blue rucksacks on their backs.

"No, Rufus!" declared the woman, grabbing the dog's collar and pulling him away. Rufus was dejected. A new person meant new smells to explore. Couldn't he take just a bit longer to sniff this inter-esting girl-child?

"Are you all right?" asked the man, offering Emily a hand and helping her to her feet, while viewing her with interest, as if she were a new artefact in a poorly lit museum.

"Are you the Ridges?" asked Emily.

"Yes." The woman smiled. "I'm Shanita and this is Frank. Who are you and what are you doing sleeping outside our front door?"

If Lady Grubnot had uttered these words they would have been laced with arsenic, but Shanita said them with a bewildered warmth.

"I'm Emily Cruet and I've travelled quite a long way to meet you and talk to you. When I got here and I saw that sign I was desperately disappointed that you were away for two weeks because there's something I urgently need to tell you and then there's somewhere I need to get back to this evening or early tomorrow morning at the latest. So I lay down on the ground and I must have fallen asleep. But I don't understand. The sign says you've gone away for two weeks from today's date."

"An ash cloud in Iceland erupted this afternoon," explained Frank.

"All flights have been suspended," added Shanita, taking the sign off the front door. "Instead of queuing for a couple of days to see if or when flights start up again, we decided to throw in the towel, pick up this grizzly mutt from the kennel people and come back home."

"The airline said we'd get a full refund so we'll go away later in the year," said Frank. "We were going to Greece and it's still warm there for the next few months."

"And anyway, maybe it's a bit of a blessing in disguise," mused Shanita. "After all, with all of those other crisp companies shutting down, there's only really us and Grubnot's Exclusives in the top end of the market. Demand has never been so high. Some friends were going to mind things on the production front while we were away but they won't need to any more."

"Would you like to come inside and talk to us about whatever it is you need to talk to us about?" asked Frank.

"Yes please," said Emily.

She instantly liked the Ridges. She loved Shanita's soft voice and the way Frank's cheeks got little dimples when he frowned.

Shanita produced a key and opened the front door, leading them into a musty-smelling passage, round a corner and into a huge open-plan kitchen. On two large wooden dressers stood faded blue-and-white crockery. There was an old black Aga range cooker and a huge wooden refectory table. The layout and the furnishings made the kitchen seem large and cosy at the same time. On the walls hung a series of intricate watercolour paintings depicting all things nautical – boats, bridges, marinas and lighthouses.

"Right," said Frank, ushering Shanita and Emily to seats at the table. "In this family we believe the answer to any problem is hot chocolate, so let me brew some up and you can tell us all about your visit here. I must say I'm intrigued."

A couple of minutes later the three of them were all cradling large white mugs filled to the brim with delicious-smelling, frothy hot chocolate. Rufus was lying in his dog basket chewing his favourite bone and making contented barking noises every now and then. Emily took a sip of hot chocolate and almost purred. It was one of the sweetest, most delectable things she had ever tasted.

"OK, Miss Emily Cruet," said Frank. "Fire away."

Emily looked confused at this turn of phrase as there didn't seem to be any guns in the vicinity and, even if there had been one, firing a bullet inside someone's kitchen didn't seem like a good idea.

"He means, you can begin," added Shanita, sensing her uncertainty.

"It's like this," said Emily. She took another sip of hot chocolate and proceeded to tell them everything that her mother had told her about Lady Grubnot's past and how her family and friends had come to live and work on the island in such a state of penury. Next, Emily talked about her childhood and described work in the production room and what she did in her free time on the island. Then she covered her chance meeting with Zak and his role in helping her leave the island, plus the arrival of the wonderful Cags. She talked for well over an hour. The Ridges listened in rapt silence, never interrupting her, their faces becoming angrier and more incensed at the worst excesses of Lady Grubnot's behaviour and schemes.

When Emily had finished, Shanita had a couple of tears snaking down her cheeks and Frank looked as if he'd just walked into a war zone.

"If what you say is true, and I have absolutely no reason to doubt you," said Frank, "then these are clearly matters for the police and the courts. The situation for you and your family is without question an example of modern-day slavery."

"You poor girl," said Shanita, touching Emily's arm. "I can't believe you've had to grow up like that."

"That's actually not the main thing I've come to talk to you about," said Emily, worrying that she might have gone in too strong with her tale, which could cause the Ridges to take rash and drastic action that could jeopardise her life and the lives of the others on the island.

"Really?" Frank frowned. "That seems more than enough for a girl your age to be dealing with. What else is there?"

Emily told them about the list she'd seen in Lady Grubnot's study and the conversation she'd heard between Lady Grubnot, Arthur Proudfoot and the Petrucis in the great hall. She also mentioned the five companies who'd ceased trading.

The Ridges faces were so pale by now they were almost translucent.

"The actions of Mr Proudfoot and Lady Grubnot in respect of those other crisp companies is industrial sabotage on a vast scale," said Sonia. "That wicked lady should end up spending the rest of her days in prison. Her poor parents."

"I think she plans to destroy your crisp-making operation next," said Emily. "You were the sixth and final company on her list and you had a question mark next to your name."

"I must say that even though the business world can be very tough, we thought those five other companies going to the sword was a bit bizarre," said Shanita, "but not in our wildest of wild dreams did we think someone was going round and deliberately breaking up those places. It's mind-blowing. It's unbelievable."

"I say we call the police and they storm the island," suggested Frank. "They'll nab her, grab all of the evidence they need from her study and free you and your fellow workers. And that will be that."

"You're forgetting what I said about all of the bombs, the trip-wired fence and most of all the emerald round her neck," replied Emily. "She would readily press that switch and blow the whole place up rather than go quietly. She wouldn't just sacrifice us; she'd sacrifice herself. However quick the police may be, Lady Grubnot would get to that emerald quicker."

"Well if we can't get the police involved because of fears for your safety, what can we do?" asked Shanita.

"The first thing must be to save your business," said Emily. "I'm pretty sure that horrible Proudfoot man will pay you a visit soon, break something vital and then return, pretend to find the fault (that he has created) and try to make you sell your business to her."

"How will we stop him?" asked Frank. "Employ guards?"

Emily shook her head. "You have to do it in a way that makes her think she has succeeded. If she knows you're onto her she'll find a way round it. She's ridiculously sly and very, very dangerous."

"If it happens in the night we might have trouble rousing ourselves," said Shanita. "We're both very heavy sleepers."

"You'll have to be on guard right round the clock," warned Emily, looking up at them with the expression of a very firm schoolteacher. "If you sleep heavily, then take turns staying up through the night. It could save your whole business."

"What do your parents say about all of this sub-terfuge?" asked Frank. "I mean, you've left the island and you've done it without them. Isn't that a very big deal for them to handle?"

Emily felt her cheeks redden. "They...they don't know about it. They're very cautious people and I'm their only child. They were nervous when I told them I was going camping on the island tonight. If they had known I was planning to come here they'd have gone completely crazy."

Emily's words hung in the air like a puff of vapour.

Shanita clasped her hands together. "What if they visit you at your tent and you're not there? They'll be beside themselves with worry, won't they? I know I would be if I were your parent."

"I think they trust me enough not to go snoop-ing. At least I hope they do."

"But you're only a child, Emily," said Frank. "You shouldn't be shouldering all of this responsibility. We're grown-ups. Stay here with us and we'll get everyone off the island."

"I told you," said Emily. "It's far too dangerous. All I need you to do at the minute, if it's OK with you, is to make sure you're ready when Mr Proudfoot or one of his minions arrives. At least that way, you'll be able to save your business."

"Fine." Shanita nodded. "We'll do as you say. But please let us help you to permanently get away from Lady Grubnot – you and everyone else on the island."

"Thank you," replied Emily. "I'm really grateful for that offer and I accept it. I just don't know at the minute what form that help might take."

"Emily," said Frank, "your story is absolutely staggering and you are a remarkable girl for managing to reach us and tell us what's going on. It should be us thanking you."

"Now I appreciate that you make the most of the mouldy vegetables Lady Grubnot pays you on the island," said Shanita, "but you're not leaving here until you've had a slap-up meal with all of the trimmings, and there won't be a soggy courgette in sight."

Emily smiled. "That's an offer I don't think I should refuse."

CHAPTER TWENTY-THREE
A MEAL LIKE NO OTHER

Frank and Shanita got to work immediately while Emily stroked Rufus. He basked in all the attention, rolling over onto his back so that she could tickle his tummy and nuzzling up to her so she'd stroke his long, soft ears. *She's all right, this one*, he thought contentedly. *Not like those children in the town the other day who stole that really interesting stick I'd tracked down.*

As pots bubbled and pans sizzled Emily felt a sense of relaxation she had never really experienced before. This was what it must feel like to be free: to sit in a kitchen stroking a dog, while others are preparing a meal, all the time bathing in the luxury of the thought that there would be no production room to work in the next day. It was so good that for a split second she entertained the possibility of never returning, but of course that was impossible. What would be the point of her enjoying her freedom when the rest of her family would probably be burnt to toast when Lady Grubnot discovered she'd escaped?

And then her thoughts turned to the coming days. Say the Ridges managed to stop Mr Proudfoot contaminating, poisoning or wrecking their crisp set-up here. What then? When Lady Grubnot discovered Proudfoot hadn't succeeded, what would she do? Would she plumb even murkier depths to get rid of her last competitors? In a frenzy of rage, would she raze Ridge Farm to a cinder? By warning them tonight might Emily be placing the Ridges in terrible danger?

"You can stop pampering that pleasure-seeking mutt now and come and get something to eat," called Frank, placing some plates and cutlery on the large farmhouse table.

The three of them sat on comfortable chairs made from wood, Emily's with a puffed-up white cushion on the seat. Soft sidelights shone warmly across the room, the oven's heat making the temperature just right, and the white dishes were elegant without being overstated. After a couple of mouthfuls Emily quickly realised she was in the presence not just of good people, but good cooks too.

The vegetable pie that came out of the oven was exquisite, as were the roast potatoes, florets of broccoli, glazed parsnips and mushroom salad that accompanied it. Each mouthful was like a brand new experience and Emily had to make herself eat slowly as opposed to guzzling as much as she could cram into her mouth.

"Another slice of pie?" asked Frank.

A second helping. This was unreal. The only second helpings they ever had back on Grubnot Island were when she and Paul could pilfer extra rations from the manor house kitchen and that was rare. Even then the seconds were tiny.

Shanita smiled. "You look like you're enjoying that."

"It's wonderful," said Emily, spearing a mushroom with her fork, a fork made out of actual metal. "It's by far the best meal I've ever had."

"You haven't had the desert yet," said Frank with a wink.

When this arrived, Emily's taste buds almost danced the tarantella. "It's apple and blackberry crumble with homemade vanilla ice cream," said Shanita, placing a giant portion in Emily's place. "Luckily, I made the crumble last night and froze it for when we came back in two weeks. Since we're back early, I heated it up, so tuck in."

The crumble was as close to divine as food can ever get and the white ball of ice cream was by far the most delicious thing Emily had ever tasted. It was what the boy in Northurst must have been eating in that cone thing.

By the time the meal was over, Emily felt as if the food had forced its way into every bone and muscle of her body, she was that full.

"Thank you so much," she said, nursing her belly.

"Once we've got you off that island, away from that horrible ogre, there will always be a place at our table for you and your family and your friends," said Shanita.

"That's really kind." Emily smiled, touched by the kindness of these people she'd only known for a couple of hours. If she didn't have her parents then Frank and Shanita would be the kind of parents she'd choose. Were all adults on the mainland this nice? She looked at the clock on the kitchen wall and saw it was nearly eleven. "I better be getting back," she said reluctantly, loathed to tear herself away from this most welcoming place.

"Are you going to phone this Zak and get him and Cags to come back and get you?" asked Frank.

Emily shook her head. "Cags had to give the taxi, or rather car, back to her brother, Bez, and Zak's mum said he had to come home or she'd ground him. I tried Cags's mobile phone but couldn't get through to her. I think I'll try again."

"You don't need to," said Shanita. "I'll be your chauffer back to Northurst. Although I'm not sure I'll be able to help you with the boat ride back to the island."

"I'm sure Zak will get me there somehow," replied Emily, who in truth hadn't given this matter much thought, so focused had she been on reaching the Ridges and imparting all of that vital information.

They all stood up and Frank shook Emily by the hand. "Emily Cruet," he said. "If in our lives we can act a tiny bit as bravely as you have acted tonight, we will be very, very proud of ourselves. You are an incredible individual and we owe you very much gratitude for your warning. The best of luck getting back to your parents and if there's anything at all, however big or small, we can do for you, then just ask and it will be done. I have a strong feeling that we will meet again."

"I hope so." Emily beamed. "It's been amazing to meet you both."

Rufus barked excitedly, thinking the small human was going to come and lie down in his basket with him for some more pampering and attention, but he was disappointed when she stroked the top of his head and then went outside with Shanita.

Round the side of the house stood an old, mud-spattered green jeep. Emily climbed up onto a small metal platform at its side so that she could reach the passenger door and climb in. Her second trip in a motor vehicle? Things worked pretty fast out here.

Down the bumpy track they went. At the gate, Shanita got out, unlocked the padlock, drove through and then relocked it. A minute later they hit the road, Emily's mind zinging with thoughts and images. She had enjoyed meeting the Ridges and Rufus, and eating their food to such a vast degree that even if she never got to leave the island again at least she'd have the memories of this incredible night.

"So what are your parents like?" asked Shanita, indicating left and turning onto a road with a sign-post indicating that Northurst was twenty-nine miles away.

"Well, my dad, Monty, is very into cooking, a bit like you two. I love it too, so we're always competing to see who can make all of those rubbish ingredients go further and who can make the tastiest meals. It's when we have fun because for eleven hours a day, Monday to Friday, we're the crisp fryers and that gets boring after a while."

Shanita smiled. "And what about your mum?"

"She's a nature person. She loves the outdoors and grows her own herbs. She likes plants and trees and I've learnt loads from her about the different ways you can use twigs and bark and reeds. We've made some great things over the last few years."

"You make things?"

"I've had a hand in creating pretty much everything in the shack over the last four or five years. I see it as a challenge. You know, taking some bits of wood and a few chunks of metal and a couple of old cardboard boxes and turning them into a sofa or a sun chair. I like working out a way to connect everything together and make a finished product. I enjoy the challenge."

"What about your granddad? You said he was there with you."

Emily went on to tell Shanita about Bob's love of chess, of Paul's love of birds and his stone collection, of Simon's practical joking and of Mel's sewing and knitting skills – taking several bits of material and concocting a new shirt or pair of trousers.

"What a talented bunch of people you are!" exclaimed Shanita. "It sounds like in the face of unbelievably harsh conditions you've created your own world over there."

"I'm not sure we're talented," replied Emily. "We just make the most of our situation. At least, that's what my parents always say."

They fell into a companionable silence for a while and then Shanita checked the time on the dashboard. "OK, we'll be at the harbour in ten minutes. Maybe try to give Cags a ring now, to see where she and Zak are."

"Good idea," said Emily. She pulled Zak's mobile phone out of her pocket and hit Cags's number. This time there was no music or alarm noises.

"Wasssupppp?" barked Cags almost instantly. The sound of shouting and furniture being thrown could be heard in the background.

"Er…it's me, Emily. Is there any way you can tell Zak to meet me at the harbour in ten minutes?"

"Consider it done," replied Cags, "I'm just fighting my brother." Emily heard something being smashed. "How did you get on with those crisp farmers?"

"They were incredibly kind and very helpful and they cooked me an amazing meal."

Shanita beamed across at her.

"I told them everything I know and they were very grateful. I'm so pleased I met them."

"Cool," said Cags. "I'll go to Zak's house and tell him to meet you. I'd love to come too but I have some unfinished business."

Emily heard Cags let out a blood-curdling roar that was followed by some ripping sounds. And then the line went dead.

When the jeep pulled into the harbour, Zak was waiting by bay three, his back resting against a street light. Shanita got out with Emily.

"Zak, this is Shanita Ridge," said Emily. "She and her husband Frank run Ridge Farm Crisps. I've warned them about Lady Grubnot's plan. They're going to do their best to stop her from closing them down and hopefully help us with some other stuff too."

"We're going to need all of the help we can get." Zak shivered. "That Lady Grubnot is one slippery enemy."

"Here, take this," said Shanita, stuffing a plastic bag under Emily's arm.

"What is it?" asked Emily.

"It's just a bit of food." Shanita smiled. "Nothing special."

"Thanks." Emily grinned. She handed Zak's mobile phone back to him.

"Take our home number as well," said Shanita, "and both mine and Frank's mobile numbers." She dictated them while Zak typed them into his phone.

"I'd love to let you hold onto my phone but my mum would kill me if she knew I'd lent it to anyone. She pays for it, as she tells me about a million times a day."

"It's probably best not to take a phone there anyway," said Emily. "If Lady Grubnot found it, who knows what she would do."

"Are you sure?" asked Zak.

Emily nodded.

"Can I give you anything else?" asked Shanita. "I feel terrible leaving you here."

"I'm fine, honestly," replied Emily. "It' been brilliant meeting you."

"When we see each other again, hopefully things might be very different," said Shanita. She gave Emily a hug, patted Zak on the shoulder and then walked back to the jeep and set off on her journey home.

"There's a problem," said Zak.

"What is it?" asked Emily, looking alarmed.

"I can't get you back to the island before tomorrow afternoon."

"Tomorrow afternoon!" gasped Emily, picturing the myriad of gigantic and possibly fatal problems this nightmare could cause her.

"All right, I'm not serious." Zak grinned, giving Emily a playful punch on the shoulder and pulling out a key with the words MR FARADAY – BOAT stamped on the label.

CHAPTER TWENTY-FOUR
QUESTIONS AND MORE QUESTIONS AND MORE... OK, YOU GET THE PICTURE

"He keeps the key under that plant pot," explained Zak, as the motor spurted to life and they pulled away from the harbour. The pot was one of several on the deck, in addition to a red-and-white life ring and a large pair of wooden oars. The deck had plenty of other space to carry the weekly load of two hundred and fifty crisp boxes.

As the boat skimmed over the dark blue surface, Emily felt cool spray dusting her body, the lapping water like a friendly sea animal popping up to make her acquaintance. She told Zak all about her conversation with the Ridges.

"They sound like really good people," said Zak. "Do you reckon you can trust them? I mean, they're not in league with Lady Grubnot are they?"

"They're totally trustworthy," replied Emily. "They were supportive, compassionate and good listeners. My only worry is that they'll be asleep when Proudfoot comes. They said they're both very heavy sleepers."

"Let's hope they have something to keep them awake," said Zak.

Emily nodded. The Ridges HAD to be awake if she stood any chance of *really* taking on Lady Grubnot.

"In all of this excitement I can't believe I haven't asked you how it's been going," said Zak.

"How what's been going?"

"The psychological groundwork we talked about. Have you had a chance to crack on with it?"

Emily laughed and then described each of her three subversions.

"That is absolutely BRILLIANT!" Zak grinned. "Well done, Emily Cruet. Excellent work. You've started softening her up. It will make her more vulnerable for when we work out a way to defeat her properly."

"It was your idea," said Emily.

"Any ideas of what to do next?"

"Not yet," replied Emily, "but I'm working on it."

"We're getting all of you off that island," said Zak. "I'm telling you."

"I agree, we just have to find the right way of doing it."

"You call the shots. You're the one in danger. When you're ready to move onto the next stage of the operation I'll be ready."

"Thanks." Emily smiled. Why were all of these people helping her? It was incredibly comforting to think of Zak, Cags and the Ridges, all of them determined to change her life and the lives of those around her. It gave her a little bit of hope, something that had always been in very short supply within her world.

The shores of the island and the huge fence encircling it approached in the distance. Zak expertly steered the boat alongside the island, some way from the south jetty and thus out of sight of anyone who happened to emerge through the island's imposing wooden gates. After tying the boat to a rock on the shore, he helped Emily off and they walked towards the gates.

"We haven't talked about how you're going to get back in, have we?" whispered Zak.

After discussing things for a few minutes, they came to the conclusion that "weird animal sounds" were probably the best re-entry device.

So Zak crept round the perimeter of the fence in the opposite direction to the boat. He then started making all sorts of braying animal noises, noises that, before long, drew Clemence down to the gate. He unlocked it and stepped towards the jetty. It was late so he hadn't had time to wear one of his outfits. He was in pyjamas, dressing gown, nightcap and slippers. Zak eased round the corner, out of sight, still barking out the bizarre sounds. As Clemence went to investigate, Emily slipped through the gate and made her way as quickly as she could in the direction of her makeshift tent.

"Pigeons," said Clemence to himself. "Wild boar?"

Zak was far faster than Clemence and therefore wasn't spotted. When he stopped making the noises, Clemence put his hands on his hips, rested for a few moments and then returned to the gate, muttering, "Owls, land-fish, otters?" He went back in, locked the gate and walked back to the manor house, scratching his head in bemusement. Zak waited a few minutes, then started the boat again and set sail for Northurst Harbour.

As Emily lay back in her rudimentary tent, with a bed of soft leaves and grass for a pillow and her blanket from the shack as a...blanket, she relived the excitement of the hours between being sealed up in the crisp box and this moment. She shuddered but laughed when she thought of Cags's mad car manoeuvres, and she was exceedingly thankful for all of the assistance Zak had heaped upon her. She was also exceptionally relieved that there'd been a volcanic eruption in Iceland so that she could meet Shanita and Frank Ridge. Hopefully, if they could prevent Mr Proudfoot from wrecking their business, Lady Grubnot's plot to destroy all of her competitors would be stopped and that could be a very significant occurrence for the seven workers on the island. This was all positive and satisfying. But even with all their all help, would it ever be truly possible to get her and the others away from Grubnot Island without being blown sky high?

As she thought about these questions, people and scenes, something suddenly hit her. She'd been off the island but there was one thing she hadn't done. How could she have been so remiss? She hadn't had any crisps. Mind you, after the feast she'd enjoyed at the Ridges, it wasn't too big a deal. There'd hopefully be other opportunities to get some. Tiredness began to take her over and her eyelids started drooping. Today was over. What would tomorrow bring?

CHAPTER TWENTY-FIVE
MR PROUDFOOT'S APPOINTMENTS

For three nights, Frank and Shanita Ridge took turns to stay up during the night hours. They sat in a chair inside their production barn and waited. But there was no sign of an intruder. No quiet footsteps, no tinkling of broken glass, no confrontation to be had. So the following night, both of them suffering from sleep deprivation, went to bed at their usual time and didn't keep guard. Unfortunately that was the very timeslot in which Arthur Proudfoot chose to strike.

The night was cloudless, a soft wind rustled the grass and the sky was a shifting cloak of blackness. Proudfoot was dressed all in black with a black beanie hat to complete his outfit. He had spent twenty minutes crouched down behind a hedge looking through high-spec binoculars to see if any signs of life were emanating from the farmhouse or the barn. But everything was dark and silent. The Ridges must have been asleep. He was alone.

Getting into their crisp-production barn was easy, ridiculously easy for Proudfoot. In fact, out of all the crisp factories he'd broken into and taken out, this was the one with the least security. To his astonishment there were no burglar alarms to shut off, no motion sensors to block, no blinking red lights to dismantle, as there had been in some of the other locations. Even the lock on the door of the barn was of pathetically low quality. He picked it in seconds and stole inside.

The people who ran this place must have been naive in the extreme. They had to be country bumpkins with not a single brain cell between them. Or they were hippies or "do-gooders" who believed that everybody in the world was good-natured and trustworthy, that no one possessed a single criminal thought. Their outlook was naive and deluded. He couldn't believe his luck. In minutes he would have sown the seeds of disaster here and when he returned shortly with his forged papers and documents he would shut them down as he had done with all of the others, and in the guise of compassion and caring would lead them straight into Lady Grubnot's outstretched clutches. And then would come his *real* payday. So far Lady Grubnot had paid him in dribs and drabs but when this job was all wrapped up she'd promised to reward him generously. And when this infusion of cash came to pass, he intended to take a break from crime and spend his ill-gotten gains; some of it on a yacht, some of it on a sports car, and use some of it just to gloat over and count.

But enough of financial projections and cash mountains, and on to the job in hand! He placed his briefcase on a steel worktop and flicked it open. Taking out a small torch he did a quick sweep of the barn and it was then that he heard a scraping noise on the ground. His body tensed. Maybe one of the Ridges had woken up by chance and seen his shadow in the barn? If that was the case, he'd need to vanish sharpish and return to complete the job another time, which would be a great inconvenience. But his torch beam alighted not on a human but rather on a canine.

A dog to you and me.

On the one hand this was fine as most dogs don't properly understand the complexities of industrial sabotage or report crimes to the forces of law and order. Plus it was a Labrador and Labs are not known as guard dogs or aggressors. On the other hand, though, it was potentially bad, as all dogs, Labrador or not, are capable of barking very loudly and of biting the limbs of interlopers should they so choose.

Proudfoot had had a dog when he was a child – Charlie, a lively cocker spaniel whom he had loved dearly. So instead of panicking or shooing the creature away, he crouched down and began murmuring, "Good boy," as he assumed it was a male. The dog looked well-groomed with a chunky metal collar sporting a white circle at the centre that gave his owners' phone number, in case he got lost. As the dog strolled over to him, Proudfoot's body tensed and he got ready to run in case this was needed, but the animal merely sniffed the air and sat down in front of him.

"Aren't you brilliant!" whispered Proudfoot, cautiously reaching out to stroke the creature on the top of his head. He seemed to like this so he stroked his ears and then the side of his face.

"I guess my luck is in, old chap," he said as the dog and he studied each other. "You could have easily started going crazy when you saw a stranger in your midst, but you didn't and for that I'm truly grateful."

The dog licked his right cheek and stared up at this portly man.

"I can't wait to tell Lady Grubnot about you." Proudfoot grinned. "She'll be tickled pink by the tale of a brain-empty mutt who sat by while I sabotaged her last high-end crisp rival. Seven crisp companies will have turned into one, just one. Think of that! Flooding, poisoning or electrical faults – we've heaped them all on her rivals and more! In days she'll have the entire market to herself. Her plan is brilliant but I assure you, my dog friend, she couldn't have done it without me. Yes, it was her idea and she's bankrolled it, but it's been me who has carried out the vital work at the crisp face, if you like. We're a team, you see – partners in crime and crisp-company destruction! Three cheers for industrial sabotage, Mr Silent Doggy!"

The dog flicked a fly off his back with his right paw.

"Well, I better be getting on," said Proudfoot. "And then I'll be off like a shadow in the night. Unseen, unheard and unrecognisable."

Reaching into his briefcase, he pulled out some screwdrivers, pliers and fuses. Crouching down under the dog's watchful eye, he opened a large white cupboard standing low on a wall and began unscrewing plugs, moving wires and replacing fuses with the ones he had brought.

"Their machines will work perfectly well and they won't notice anything until I return for a snap inspection tomorrow morning," he informed the dog when he'd completed his task. "Examining their electrical points and systems, I will find a set-up so haphazard, so dangerous, that I will, with great sadness, be forced to make them stop trading. How sad. What a shame; another production unit gone, another fire sale to Lady Grubnot!"

He stood up, placed his tools back into the briefcase and took a quick look around the barn, making sure he hadn't left any trace of himself. Then he stroked the dog's head again and exited. After relocking the padlock and congratulating himself on his superb work, he hurried away into the night, laughing out loud when he thought of the docile dog who had watched him but done nothing.

❖ ❖ ❖

And true to form, Arthur Proudfoot returned to Ridge Farm the following morning. And the Ridges, who had slept during his operation in the night, were just as devastated as the Petrucis and the five other shattered company owners had been when he told them of the grave faults he'd uncovered in their operation.

"But surely we can shut down for a few days and redo the wiring," pleaded Shanita, close to tears.

"We have a great electrician," said Frank. "We could have the place fixed by the end of the week."

"I appreciate that," said Mr Proudfoot, "I really do. But IPSRA has very strict safety guidelines and, as your standards have fallen so low beneath what we consider is a reasonable threshold, I have no option other than to serve you with a notice to cease trading."

"But this company is our lives," cried Shanita. "We've plunged all of our life savings into it. If you close us down we'll have nothing."

"There is a possible route to salvage some of your money," said Mr Proudfoot thoughtfully. "I may be able to facilitate the sale of your company, with all of its problems attached, to another player in the upper-end crisp market."

"Really?" asked an ashen-faced Frank. "Who is it?"

He listened to the caller for a few minutes and then ended the call.

"I'll make some enquiries and get back to you very shortly," replied Proudfoot with a very heavy sigh. "It breaks my heart to see fine people like your-selves in such trying circumstances. I will do every-thing in my power to secure the best price for you. I will fight your corner, believe me."

"That's so kind of you, Mr Proudfoot," said Shanita. "We hope you find someone quickly."

"I have no doubt that I will," said Proudfoot kindly, shaking them both by the hand. "I will be in touch very soon."

As he began his walk back down the track towards his car, he was sure he could detect the sound of weeping behind him.

Chapter Twenty-Six
Overheard and
Understood

"So can you pay me the full whack now?"

"Not quite yet – there is one more stage of my plan to be enacted."

It was the following afternoon and Emily had taken a short break. She was inside the decrepit outdoor toilet next to the production room when she heard the voices of Lady Grubnot and that horrible Mr Proudfoot outside.

"But you said you'd pay me the final sum when all of your competitors were destroyed and that objective has been achieved. Ridge Farm was the last of the six and I have crushed its owners. We will stage one last meeting here at the island with you on Sunday and once you have bought them out the project will be completely finished. So payment now would be greatly appreciated."

"My meeting with the Ridges will have to take place after Sunday, Mr Proudfoot, because on Sunday we have bigger crisps to fry."

"Another high-end crisp company to ruin? I thought they were all spoken for?"

"No, Mr Proudfoot, I am talking of a far bigger job; something stupendous, something unique, something up at Farham Castle."

Emily's ears seemed to swivel like antennae. Farham Castle? That was one of the royal palaces; it was where Zak said his cousin Martin worked.

"At the castle? I'm not sure I get you."

"Let me tell you something, Mr Proudfoot. Those royals love posh crisps. They can't get enough of them. So on Sunday they are going to be served a new flavour that will totally blow their minds."

Emily kept rigidly still. This sounded like a fascinating conversation and she didn't want them to be alerted to her presence.

"Are they produced by Ridge Farm?"

"No, because a message has made its way to them that Ridge Farm is about to run into all sorts of problems and their crisps must be avoided at all costs."

"Well they can't come from here. You said the royals will never, ever buy Grubnot's Exclusives because of the animosity that exists between you."

"Correct."

"So how are they going to get their hands on any posh crisps when there's no company to buy them from? Are they going to get them from abroad?"

"Absolutely not. There is another way."

"There is?"

Emily listened with intense concentration. What was Lady Grubnot up to now? What wickedness was she planning? What was she going to ask Mr Proudfoot to do this time?

"What if I single-handedly, without the knowledge or involvement of any of my snivelling workers, produced some specially flavoured crisps under a new company name, a company that is untraceable to me? And what if I've arranged things so that the royals have already placed an order with this company? What if I could use this company to exact my ultimate revenge?"

She lowered her voice and whispered some words to Proudfoot. Emily strained to hear them but they were too quiet.

"That is outlandish!" gasped Proudfoot. "It's scandalous! Can we really pull it off?"

Emily heard the rustling of a piece of paper.

"The sum I have written down here is the amount I will pay you if you help me bring this spectacular final ruse to fruition. You will see that it is five times more than we originally agreed for the ruination of my rivals."

Arthur Proudfoot let out a high-pitched squeal, like a small child ripping off wrapping paper and discovering the present of his dreams.

"What will be my role?" he asked, saliva audibly dripping from the side of his mouth.

"I will do the preparation on Sunday morning," said Lady Grubnot briskly. "You will arrive at the island by ten a.m. You will get the crisps to the castle well before the twelve p.m. start of luncheon. You will get in using a set of forged papers I have acquired on your behalf. You will deliver the product *in person* and oversee the final stage of the mission. I will then be in pole position and you will return here to collect your takings."

"With such a dangerous brief, might there be any way of upping the amount you just showed me?" asked Proudfoot. "After all, if I'm caught they won't let me off lightly."

"Don't be greedy, Mr Proudfoot. Just play your part, come here at ten on Sunday, and collect your cash when the deed is done."

"I will start making preparations at once, Lady Grubnot," said Proudfoot, knowing that he could push the Lady no further on price.

"Off you go, Mr Proudfoot. Great things await us!"

The noise of footsteps sounded and their voices drifted out of earshot.

Emily sat there for several minutes trying to figure out what this conversation had been about.

A company that is untraceable to me.

They are going to be served a new flavour that will totally blow their minds.

I will then be in pole position.

What did it all mean? How were these concepts connected? What was Lady Grubnot plotting that could be bigger than closing down all her rivals? And then Emily remembered the empty box labelled BERKSHIRE CRISPS that she and Paul had seen in the pantry.

Berkshire Crisps. *A company that is untraceable to me.*

Why would Lady Grubnot get involved with another company? She hated other companies. Was this Berkshire company from another country? Did she have some kind of stake in it?

"Emily, are you in there?" It was her mother's voice, sounding pinched and anxious.

Emily scooted back outside and ran towards Janet.

"Everything OK?" asked Janet.

"Totally." Emily said. "Back to the grindstone."

Janet gave her a funny look but said nothing.

❧   ❧   ❧

After a game of chess that night with Bob (Emily won despite Bob's hardest efforts), they got to talking about Pirate Summers as they often did.

"Do you think there's good and bad in Pirate Summers?" asked Emily, after they'd cleared away the chess set and were sitting at the table. She was fixated on the conversation she'd overheard earlier and was trying to figure out not only what it meant but whether or not the whole Lady Grubnot story was as completely one-sided as she'd thought. Aside from her competitor-crushing antics, when it came to the royals was there a possibility that she was just trying to make a statement about what she saw as her unjust treatment at their hands?

"There's good and bad in everyone," said Bob, tracing a line of wood on the table with his finger.

"Do you really think so? What about Lady Grubnot?"

"Ah, that's a difficult one. I can't see anything good in her now but maybe when she was younger she had the odd good thought or carried out the occasional small task of positivity here and there."

172

"Maybe." Emily shivered since she, of course, thanks to her mum and unbeknownst to Bob, now had a pretty clear picture of Lady Grubnot's life and times.

"You asked about Pirate Summers?"

Emily nodded.

"Well, remember the scene where he needs to take control of that ravine, the one that's guarded by the nomadic people."

"He has to take control of it or he'll never stop the motley crew of palace guards," said Emily.

"Correct," said Bob. "He has to take *control*. What does he do about it?"

"At first he thinks he'll have to fight them but when he realises they're willing to negotiate he talks to them and they work out a deal that will suit them both."

"You said it." Bob nodded. "He *ends up* negotiating with them but his initial thought was of a confrontation. However much we're rooting for him, this first thought could be viewed as 'bad' or 'negative'. He was prepared to wipe them all out if necessary to achieve his goal."

As soon as these words left Bob's mouth an ugly notion suddenly entered Emily's brain. It was a notion about Lady Grubnot, Proudfoot, Farham Castle and the discussion Emily had overheard just a few hours ago.

No, she thought, her hand involuntary going over her mouth in disbelief. *No!*

"What's up?" asked Bob, seeing her expression change so radically. "Do you think you should have beaten me in less moves?"

"No. I'm just tired. I need a lie-down."

"Suit yourself, young lady, and well played."

Emily staggered over to her bed in a trance, ignoring everything that was going on around her, the idea building and transforming by the moment. She was convinced that the meaning of Lady Grubnot's *ultimate* plan had suddenly crystallised in her mind like a jumbled-up Rubik's cube deftly twisted to colour perfection. Forget unfair treatment; forget being an outcast. This was unjustifiable. This was very, very, very bad.

In fact this was on a different planet.

This was murder.

CHAPTER TWENTY-SEVEN
A DRASTIC TURN

"You must be joking!" gasped Zak when Emily met him at their usual spot after work on Saturday.

In the hours and minutes since she'd pieced Lady Grubnot's plan together she had done nothing else other than think of a way to stop it.

"You're in your own world at the minute, aren't you?" Janet had observed during their very short lunch break. She'd tried to strike up a conversation with Emily about possible designs for a new workbench for the porch, but Emily hadn't responded, not even with a one-word answer.

But now, with Zak on the other side of the fence, she couldn't stop talking.

"I'm not joking. By getting rid of all her competitors, she's taken complete control of the posh-crisps market."

"But you've told me that the royal family won't touch her stuff."

"They won't. That's why she's set up a brand new company going by the name of Berkshire Crisps. I'm sure of it."

"But surely the royal family will know she's behind it."

"They won't. She's probably gone to immense lengths to conceal her involvement. I overheard her saying she was going to make the crisps herself without any of her workers involved. She must have covered her tracks so well that the royals will never suspect."

"And these Berkshire Crisps? You say they're going to be…"

"She said she was going to 'totally blow the minds' of the royal family and then take 'pole position' for herself. I'm pretty sure she meant she's going to poison the crisps, take out the royal family in one go and then, as she'll be the closest living heir to the throne, she'll become Queen."

"But that's horrific!" cried Zak. "It's treason. It's a lock-you-up-in-the-Tower-of-London-and-throw-away-the-key job. Are you absolutely sure about this?"

"As sure as anyone can be about anything after eavesdropping on a planning meeting, but it does all make sense. As she said, it would be her ultimate revenge for the way the royals banished her all those years ago. She despises them with every sharp-pointed bone in her body."

"If what you say is true, this time we really have to bring in the police."

"No!" shot back Emily. "You know the danger my family is in. I get it that everyone on the mainland wants to get the police involved but you and I have to do this this alone."

"But this is too big for us. It's gigantic. It'll go down in history textbooks after Guy Fawkes and the gunpowder plot."

"Guy Fawkes?"

"Don't worry about him, worry about what we can do."

"So you're willing to help with this? You're in?"

"Of course I am!" thundered Zak. "What do we do to start?"

"I think it should go like this," said Emily, and she quickly outlined her plan.

CHAPTER TWENTY-EIGHT
DRAWINGS AND PLANS

"Come in!" called a voice.

Emily opened the door to Clemence's inventing room. He was sitting at his desk, entangled in lots of orange string and trying to release himself. His wooden chest was open and hundreds of multicoloured items were spilled out over its side. There was a musty, ashy smell as if Clemence had recently built an indoor bonfire. A range of small hammers and pliers were scattered over his desk's work surface and two large coffee mug stains had appeared at the edge nearest him, like two eyes, monitoring the rhythms and flows of his inventing activities.

"Good evening," he said. "You couldn't give me a hand to break free from my soon-to-be-patented never-ending yo-yo, could you?"

"Of course," replied Emily. It was a matter of moments before she'd freed him. "What's a yo-yo?"

"It's a disc connected to a length of string. You manipulate the disc's movements by moving the string around, dropping it, swinging it and throwing it out from your body."

"Sounds great," said Emily.

"This one's still in its teething stages," sighed Clemence, "but I will crack it. I've always wanted a yo-yo that never stopped."

"How would you work it at night when you're asleep?" asked Emily, studying the disc with interest and noting how the string was wrapped round its central shaft. "Would you hang it off your bed or something?"

"Excellent idea! I just have to get it *started* before I can go any further."

"Er, Clemence, can I ask you a question?"

"Of course." Clemence nodded, placing the yo-yo down on one of the coffee stains. "What can I do for you?"

"I was wondering. Do you have any maps or plans of the island, especially anything relating to the buildings?"

Clemence's face scrunched up as he thought this over. "I do have *some* plans but they're very, very old. Why are you interested in them?"

"I love to discover the layout of places, especially old ones. Knowing how things were designed can be a very great asset to an inventor."

"I totally agree" Clemence smiled. "What an insightful observation."

Standing up, he opened a tall faded brown cupboard. Several files and documents fell out, producing clouds of thick dust.

"Sorry about this," coughed Clemence. "It's been a while since I looked in here."

After rummaging around for a couple of minutes, he pulled out a roll of documents that were held together by two rubber bands. Off came the bands before he placed the documents on his desk. The first few were illustrations of Grubnot Island: the contours of the land, the measurements of the paths, the circumference of the estate. The next two related to the wartime activities carried out here, detailing elements of the bomb-making process and the primitive accommodation constructed for the makers of these ground-busting mechanisms. But with the next batch Emily felt a crackle of excitement.

That was because these were architectural drawings of every building on the island. Emily pretended to be interested in the drawings of the manor house from various elevations, but the one that she desperately needed to observe, the one that she was now holding, was a detailed plan of the mixing tower.

It said on the paper that this had originally been designed as a grain store, but that didn't matter. What mattered was the fact that the architect had drawn all of the dimensions, and every air duct, pipe and supporting pillar.

She couldn't ask Clemence if she could borrow the drawing, because he might innocently say something to Lady Grubnot about this arrangement, so she pored over it, trying to commit as many details as possible to memory.

When she'd done this, she spent time looking at plans for some of the other buildings as a further ruse to divert Clemence away from her focus on the mixing tower.

It was dark outside by the time she had taken in as much as she needed and, after thanking Clemence profusely, she hurried back to the shack, images of pipes, foundation stones and entry points zipping through her head.

CHAPTER TWENTY-NINE
THE MIXING TOWER

Emily woke just after 8 a.m. on Sunday. At first her mind was blank but quickly she remembered that this was THE MOST IMPORTANT DAY OF HER LIFE. After grabbing a couple of crackers and some home-pressed orange juice (made in the juicer she'd created with a few oranges pilfered from the manor house), she told her half-awake father that she was going for a stroll. Before she set off she grabbed a candle and matches from the kitchenette, a trowel from the porch, a stone from the path outside the shack, and a small screwdriver and bolt cutters she'd "borrowed" from Clemence's inventing room.

As we know, the mixing tower was tall and circular. It stood on top of a sloping grass mound with its bottom buried deep in the ground. Circling the entire structure was a fence topped with barbed wire. A locked metal gate was set into the fence and a large wooden door was the only visible entry point to the building. But Emily only took a cursory look at these. She walked around the outside of the fence, an image of Clemence's map laid out in her mind. When she reached the spot she was looking for, she quickly cut a small hole in the fence round the back of the building, hoping Lady Grubnot would not spot this. Slipping through the fence, she got down on her hands and knees and started digging in the grass slope with the trowel. After a couple of false starts, the third place she dug achieved the result she was seeking.

The trowel hit something hard. Working with the gardening implement and her fingers for ten minutes, she finally uncovered a metal manhole cover. It took all of her strength to prise it up, but when she did so, she saw the start of a dark, hollow space underneath. This was the opening to the tunnel she'd spied on the architectural drawings.

Replacing as much of the mud and grass that she'd dug up on top of the manhole cover, she eased herself into the darkness and pulled the cover shut.

Emily lit her candle. The tunnel had smooth stone walls bearing scratch marks. It was just about big enough for her to crawl along. She moved as quickly as she could, conscious that time was limited and that Lady Grubnot could arrive at any moment.

The tunnel sloped upwards with the contours of the grass mound. Where the mound ended, the tunnel continued inside the brickwork of the building. It took Emily seven minutes of hard labour to reach the top and find, as expected, a meshed metal vent in front of her. She used the screwdriver to undo the vent and placed it against the wall of the tunnel. She found herself looking down into the insides of the mixing tower.

This was a large circle of space with a tiled black floor and tall floor lamps placed at regular intervals along the walls, creating a slightly harsh light. In the middle of the room stood a large chrome work surface. A whole series of white pipes snaked in all directions across the ceiling, some lying flat, others sloping downwards. Stretching all the way round the circular walls was a collection of long light-grey shelves, on which sat hundreds of vials, each filled with a liquid or powder seasoning, each with a white label on its front. When Emily squinted she could read some of the labels. Some were straightforward seasonings, like "Salt" and "Balsamic Vinegar", and some were plain bizarre, like "Burnt Chocolate and Goose Liver" and "Goat's Cheese Horseradish".

On an orange storage unit next to the shelves were rows and rows of the silver crucibles in which Lady Grubnot mixed these seasonings to make her crisp flavours. Emily had seen plenty of these in the production room. Lady Grubnot was forever taking them to the seasoning cupboard, in which she added these mixed seasonings to her crisps.

An archway on the far side of the mixing tower led to another room, this one seemingly much smaller. When she leant forward, Emily could see some black filing cabinets in this second room, as well as a desk and a telephone. It looked like an administrative space in addition to the study, for Lady Grubnot's crisp-making operations, reasoned Emily.

She took in all of these features, and then she waited.

Twenty minutes later, she heard the fence door being unlocked, pushed open and shut again, and then a key twist in the tower's wooden door. From Emily's heightened perch she watched in fascination as Lady Grubnot entered the room, headed for the orange unit, and pulled down an empty silver crucible. She carried this to the work surface. Then she made for the grey shelves and collected two vials. One was labelled "Chicken Skin", the other "Marjoram". She then produced a third vial from her jacket pocket; this one was labelled "Odourless/Tasteless/Untraceable Poison", with a skull and crossbones sitting just below the words.

Even though Emily was pretty sure she'd been right about Lady Grubnot's plan, it still chilled her to the core to see this third bottle, because now this wasn't just some fantasy in her head; this was real. And if Lady Grubnot got her way, as a result of this third ingredient, some very real human beings would soon be really very dead.

Lady Grubnot started muttering out loud about the pain in her neck, the blockage in her ears and an issue with her vision.

"I can't let these things bother me!" she hissed at herself. "Get on with your work, Wilhelmina!"

She emptied out some chicken-skin powder, sprinkled a handful of crushed marjoram and dropped a substantial dose of the poisonous liquid into the silver crucible. She began mixing these ingredients with a wooden spoon and that was when Emily made her move, knowing that her timing would be the difference between life and death, not just for the royal family but for her too. One thing was incredibly clear to Emily as large doses of adrenaline kicked in. Stopping Lady Grubnot from doing what she was attempting to do wouldn't free Emily and the other workers, but it would save some other people's lives and it *had* to be done. In short, the Lady could not leave this tower with that crucible.

Pushing the top half of her body over the lip of the tunnel as far as it could safely go, Emily grabbed hold of the nearest horizontal white ceiling pipe. She gripped it tightly and started to move along it, her legs swinging in the air beneath her. Lady Grubnot carried on with her grating humming and her mixing, totally unaware that one of her workers was hanging in the air, some ten metres above her. At the end of the pipe, Emily reached for another one, this one longer in length and sloping downwards.

She progressed slowly, keen to make no noise, determined to make sure Lady Grubnot had no pre-text to look up. At the end of this pipe, she switched to another horizontal pipe. The nerves were making her entire body tremble and she was thankful for not wearing any jewellery because this would have rattled like an overnight train zipping through some countryside. The pipe ended and she prepared her-self to grasp a second downwards one. This would end in a position from where she could make her final move. But this last pipe was incredibly hot and as soon as her fingers touched it she had to let go to avoid being scalded. In that split second Emily Cruet went crashing down, straight towards the top of Lady Grubnot's head.

CHAPTER THIRTY

THE TERROR, THE TASK AND THE TREMENDOUS TROUBLE

As Emily's body hurtled downwards she threw out her arms in sheer panic and her right hand just managed to grab a parallel downwards pipe, this one thankfully stone cold.

And there she dangled.

Not more than three metres above her wicked employer. Her left hand had joined her right hand. They were gripping this cold pipe for dear life.

Worryingly, her sharp intake of breath at this unexpected shock and the clang of her grabbing the saviour pipe were both loud enough to grab the Lady's attention. Lady Grubnot's head lifted and Emily was sure it was about to end in tears, oceans of them. But mercifully the Lady was so engrossed in her nefarious task that her eyes remained glued to the workbench and the silver crucible.

Steadying both her body and her nerves, Emily very carefully withdrew the stone from her pocket just as Lady Grubnot was completing her mixing process and throwing the wooden spoon into a small see-through container. Emily held the pipe with her right hand and threw the stone over Lady Grubnot's head with her left, under the archway and into the admin room. It made a loud clanging sound and then several *clop, clop, clops* as it bounced over the floor.

Lady Grubnot froze and grimaced with suspicion. She touched her strained neck. Was she hearing things again? "What was that?" she muttered angrily to herself. And then, just as Emily had hoped, this poison-concocting villain stomped off to the admin room to discover the source of this irritating noise.

This was Emily's chance. Letting go of the pipe she landed on the mixing tower floor. She grabbed the poison mix crucible from the work surface and rushed over to the shelving units, passing Lady Grubnot who had her back to Emily and was nosily pulling open filing cabinets in the admin room.

Emily stood the poison-containing crucible back on the crucible shelf and grabbed an empty one.

"What was it – an imaginary noise?" hissed Lady Grubnot, pulling open some cupboards, taking a look inside them and then slamming their doors. She clearly hadn't seen the stone.

Emily snatched a vial marked "Mineral Water" and headed back, spying Lady Grubnot throwing open an admin-room window and looking outside. Emily tiptoed back past her and placed the new crucible on the work surface in roughly the same place Lady Grubnot's crucible had stood. With shaking fingers, Emily tipped some of the chicken-skin powder and marjoram into this new crucible.

Then she poured in some mineral water to a level she hoped would resemble the same Lady Grubnot had reached. Frenziedly stirring this mixture with a finger, she heard Lady Grubnot now kicking a cupboard in the admin room. "Did I hear it or didn't I hear it!" she was shouting in exasperation.

Emily then heard the sound of papers being rustled. It was time to go. At rapid pace, she climbed up onto the work surface and grabbed hold of the cold pipe that had saved her.

Emily knew time was now desperately limited. Lady Grubnot would give up her search very soon and return to the main room. She had to get out of here.

The arrival journey had been largely downhill. The return would be mainly upward and would thus be physically much harder.

Pulling herself up the cold pipe, Emily's arms immediately started aching. *Forget the strain, this is only my first pipe*, she instructed herself.

"It's ridiculous!" shouted Lady Grubnot, smacking one of the filing cabinets shut.

Emily grabbed a horizontal pipe and pulled herself along it, stealing quick glances down for signs of the Lady.

Next was a long uphill pipe and this was tough. Her arms were now aching like crazy and she heard Lady Grubnot scream, "WHAT WAS IT?"

Reaching the end of the up pipe, a terrified Emily now had just one final pipe to go along and then she'd be safe. But as Lady Grubnot's clanking shoes hit the admin floor in fury, a terrible situation now faced Emily.

Leaving the tunnel had been easy – she'd just slid out. Getting back into it was going to be another matter. She swung on the pipe to try to get her legs over the edge of the tunnel opening but she couldn't make it. Her arms were groaning, her mind was racing, her fate was hanging in the balance, and not just figuratively.

Panic crashed over her as the clanking footsteps of Lady Grubnot started moving. Swinging again, Emily's legs once more missed the tunnel.

"I'll get my ears, eyes and neck examined at the same time," growled Lady Grubnot. "I'll choose a weak-mannered doctor who'll accept a meagre payment!"

The footsteps were now marching towards the archway.

Emily knew she had a few seconds at most and realised with horror that even if she could swing her legs over the opening, propelling herself back into it would be a phenomenal struggle.

But she didn't give up.

With a Herculean effort she finally managed to get her legs over the lip, but her arms were so leaden and painful she didn't have enough strength to get the rest of her body in. She hung there, half in, half out.

"Back to business!" declared Lady Grubnot, reaching the threshold between the two rooms.

This was it.

Exposed.

A sitting, or in this case swinging, target.

But as Lady Grubnot's clanking feet stomped into the main room, a pair of hands suddenly shot out from the top of the tunnel and grabbed Emily by the elbows. She let go of the pipe as her body was pulled into the vent, a millisecond before Lady Grubnot reappeared.

CHAPTER THIRTY-ONE
THE CRISPS' JOURNEY BEGINS

"Another noise!" blurted out Lady Grubnot, referring to a second clanging sound she'd just heard. This one had been caused by Emily's back whacking against the side of the tunnel when she was pulled through the opening. "Are these real or am I hearing things?" The Lady gazed up at the mixing-tower lights and the mass of sprawling pipes. A moment earlier and she'd have spotted Emily. The Lady sighed. Everything looked in order. She shook her head, which hurt her neck, and returned to the work surface.

"Be calm, Wilhelmina," she ordered herself. "The hour of glory is nearly upon me."

She grabbed a crucible lid, screwed it onto the crucible Emily had prepared and stormed towards the door, clutching the seasoning as if were a newborn chick.

At the top of the tunnel, Emily gazed at Paul in wonder.

"I'm really sorry but I followed you," he whispered. "I just wanted to know what you were doing."

"Sorry?" panted Emily. "You don't have to be sorry. You just saved me."

CRISPS

Paul beamed proudly. "So are you going to tell me what it is you're up to now?"

"Yes." Emily nodded. "But first we need to get out of here. I'll explain everything on the way."

By the time Emily and Paul had climbed out of the tunnel, pushed open the manhole cover and replaced it, Lady Grubnot was long gone and Emily had outlined her plan.

"Right now, Lady Grubnot will be in the production room making a batch of crisps to which she'll add the non-poisonous seasoning I just swapped for the deadly one," she explained to Paul.

"So due to your efforts, every packet that goes into that Berkshire box will be totally safe and the royal family can eat them?" asked Paul.

"Exactly. They'll be as safe as any other crisps ever made on this island. The royals can eat them and my plan to topple Lady Grubnot can still go ahead."

"It's brilliant." Paul grinned. "Is there anything else I can do to help?"

Emily nodded. "Definitely. A bit later I'll need you down at the south jetty."

"Consider it done," said Paul, giving Emily a Pirate Summers salute.

They reached the fork in the path near the shack. "OK," said Emily, "you go back to bed before the adults get up from their Sunday lie-ins. If they see me gone they'll probably be fine about it. They know I like to do stuff by myself sometimes. If they see us both gone they'll probably get suspicious."

"No problem," said Paul.

193

"Thanks for your sterling efforts back there – you were amazing" said Emily. "Let's catch up later."

Paul hurried back to the shack while Emily ran the other way, up to the production room.

Peering through the broken window, she saw Lady Grubnot emerge from the seasoning cupboard a few minutes later. The Berkshire box of crisps was out of view but Emily could see some crisp packets with the Berkshire logo.

Clemence arrived a short time later. He and the Lady moved off to the loading bay and the forklift, which were out of Emily's view.

It's fine, she thought. *I'll race down to the south jetty and wait for them out of sight. When the box is loaded onto the boat, I can relax, knowing the diners up at Farnham Castle will be safe at their lunch. Then we'll move on to the final stage.*

She darted back down the side of the production room and sprinted along a different path to the one the forklift would take. Arriving near the south jetty, she hid behind a tree a short way along the path.

The forklift announced its wheezy arrival a little while later and Clemence dismounted. Lady Grubnot had sat beside him for the journey and she dismounted too. Clemence unlocked the main gates and Mr Proudfoot walked through. He had arrived on a boat he had rented for the day, with the express purpose of getting the Berkshire box to the royal family. Emily couldn't see the crisp box but she knew it would be there. *Just get it onto the boat and take it away*, thought Emily.

"Everything in order?" asked Mr Proudfoot.

"This batch of crisps will be especially delicious." Lady Grubnot grinned. "Good luck to those who taste them!"

They won't need good luck. Those crisps are totally harmless.

"Bring them out, Clemence!" ordered the Lady.

"As you wish." Clemence nodded and reached down to the blades of the truck.

But Emily's throat constricted and her stomach slam-dunked in horror as Clemence handed Mr Proudfoot not one box of Berkshire Crisps, but *two*.

CHAPTER THIRTY-TWO
DEFEAT IN THE COURT OF THE ROYALS

For a second Emily considered jumping out from her hiding place, running at Proudfoot, snatching the two boxes and throwing them into the sea, but he was already putting them on the boat and revving the engine. And if she did reveal herself, Lady Grubnot would see her and hell would raise its beastly head.

She'd told Zak yesterday that by the time the crisps reached Farham Castle they'd be absolutely poison free – she would make sure that it happened. She'd *promised* him. But Lady Grubnot must have prepared another batch of Berkshires earlier in the morning or at some stage yesterday. She and Paul had seen a single Berkshires box in the pantry, so she'd assumed Mr Proudfoot would be leaving with just one. She hadn't considered for one second that there might be more. So she hadn't said anything to Zak. He would naturally assume that both boxes were fine and would allow the royals to munch on them quite happily. And now, with Mr Proudfoot's boat chugging away, there was nothing she could do. All of her efforts had been for nothing. Very soon the royals would be suffering grisly deaths and Lady Grubnot would have won!

In a state of abject misery and bone-sapping despair, Emily walked back to the manor house and shuffled up the fire escape steps at the back. Yes, there would hopefully be a chance now to expose Lady Grubnot's dirty deeds in the crisp business, but how insignificant would that be when the entire royal family would be dead? Emily had switched a crucible, and she'd "softened up" Lady Grubnot by playing psychological games on her, but so what? The bigger picture was laden with doom, making Emily feel tiny, helpless and insignificant. With drooping shoulders and grief in her heart, she shuffled into Clemence's inventing room.

Clemence's desk was covered with several new designs for his soon-to-be-patented never-ending yo-yo. Emily knelt down on the floor, grabbed an item and stood up again. *Surely*, she told herself, *there's no point in doing what I'm about to do? My plan has failed. It's wretched. Rotten. A humiliation.* But something inside her made her press on even though she knew it was futile.

Knowing that Lady Grubnot hardly ever left the island, Emily was sure she'd be controlling today's operations from the manor house. So Emily trudged down to the third floor and listened at the door of the study. Silence.

Opening the door, she quickly slipped inside and crossed the frayed carpet. Getting down on all fours she crawled into the space behind the tatty green sofa, pulling the item she'd borrowed from Clemence's inventing room in beside her. She then shuffled her body around until she was as comfortable as possible, although this manoeuvre did nothing to alleviate the sense of dread that continued to rise in her chest.

Ten minutes later she heard the familiar clanking footsteps and, peering out a tiny bit from her hiding place, she saw the door being flung open and Lady Grubnot enter, a look of exhilarated anticipation stretched all over the contours of her face, a giggle bursting from her lips. She walked over to her mahogany writing desk and sat down. Making a steeple with her fingers, she sat there chuckling to herself.

If only I'd thought there might be another box. Maybe I could have stopped all of this.

Twelve o'clock passed and still Lady Grubnot sat there, grinning to herself and making excited sounds.

Finally, at 12.17 p.m., the Lady pushed a button on the table and a large wooden panel on one of the study walls slid back to reveal a big screen. It had black edges and a small camera fixed to its top so that Lady Grubnot could post pictures of herself, as well as receiving images.

The screen flickered to life and Emily gazed up at it. It showed the gigantic dining hall at Farham Castle, with huge cream drapes hanging from the windows, a deep golden carpet and elegant semicircular art-deco glass lights hanging from the ceiling. There was Mr Proudfoot standing to the side of a very long dining table, grinning with delight into the camera on the laptop he had set up.

Emily directed her gaze over Mr Proudfoot's shoulder and a sharp, icy clasp scrunched up her stomach muscles. For there, in the dining hall behind him, were all whom she assumed were the key members of the royal family. Some were slumped over the large table, their eyes frozen in horror, their skin pallid and lifeless. Others lay face down on the carpet, their bodies listless and lifeless, while another lot were crumpled over low tables or upturned chairs that must have been knocked over in the last agonising seconds of their existence.

What an awful way to die.

The poison must have hit them and worked fast. Just as she had feared, Lady Grubnot's extra box of Berkshire Crisps had done the job.

All was lost.

And while unmasking Lady Grubnot's sabotage operations was possible, Emily hadn't had time to turn her thoughts to ways of proving that Lady Grubnot had poisoned those crisps. She'd been focusing too hard on saving the lives of the royal family to do that. And now they were dead, no one would ever be able to trace this murderous crime back to the Lady's doorstep. Emily had no photo or film of what Lady Grubnot had done in the mixing tower. And the poison was odour free and undetectable.

Lady Grubnot stood up and, with a majestic flourish of her arm, walked right up to the screen, her lips quivering. "I have waited such a very long time for this moment, Mr Proudfoot," she said triumphantly, a blazing fire of desire in her cunning eyes. "I can never forgive or forget the way the royal family have treated me over the years. As a young and innocent child I was banished from their midst like a leper, and for what? Smearing a bit of ice cream over a sofa, answering back to an adult who ordered me to apologise to their son or daughter because I'd lightly tapped them on the head with a croquet mallet, and smashing a few overpriced glass and china heirlooms? My parents didn't support me one iota in attempting to overturn this ruling; from the day of my banishment *they* continued to attend each and every royal event to which they were invited. This filled me with rage and bitterness, feelings that have never left me, until now. Today, Mr Proudfoot, revenge is finally mine. The royals have had their comeuppance for the wanton cruelty they heaped on me. They have paid with their lives. This moment is mine and I will relish it for the rest of my days. Justice has finally been done! Don't you think so, Mr Proudfoot?"

Proudfoot took a small reverential bow and replied, "Yes, *Your Majesty.*"

CHAPTER THIRTY-THREE
A MIRACLE

Revulsion and anger frothed inside Emily. This monstrous woman had just murdered the entire royal family. Forget heirs one, two and three. She'd done away with the lot of them and plenty more. And as Lady Grubnot was next in line to the throne, she was in "pole position", just as she had planned. Emily knew almost nothing about the royal family but she understood that becoming Queen was a remarkably big deal. With a multitude of royal powers at her disposal, the notion of Emily and the others ever being free had just been extinguished like a match in a rainstorm. Emily was completely crushed and felt like curling up in a ball where she was and remaining there for as long as she could.

What should have been the best day of my life has turned into the WORST day of my life!

But as Emily stared at the screen in utter despair and distress, something rather wonderful suddenly happened behind Mr Proudfoot.

Prince Oliver, who was halfway down the table, his face buried in a large silver salad bowl, suddenly raised his head a fraction.

It was an act that made Emily, Lady Grubnot and Arthur Proudfoot all recoil in shock.

Very slowly the prince sat up, gazed at Proudfoot's laptop camera and said, "Those crisps had a delightful new flavour. Tangy and salty but very luckily not DEADLY!"

Proudfoot had to grip the back of a chair to prevent himself keeling over. Lady Grubnot let out a horror-stricken gasp. Emily stuck her head further out from her hiding place, her agony suddenly evaporating. Were the royals given some kind of wonder injections as children that had just brought them back from the dead? Had someone plied them with an antidote?

As Emily was marvelling over the prince's re-entry into the land of the living, Princess Annabel, who was lying on the carpet, her legs and the train of her dress sprawled over a low coffee table, raised her body off the floor and now *she* faced the camera. "I think that poisoning snack foods served to the royal family with the intention of killing them probably falls under the heading of TREASON," she noted pointedly.

Proudfoot yelped in horror.

"This...this...this can't be happening," croaked Lady Grubnot.

"Oh yes it can!" declared King Harold in a mock pantomime voice, lifting his head out of a tureen of soup and wiping his face clean with a napkin. "Thought you'd wiped us all out, didn't you, Wilhelmina? Destroyed all of your crisp rivals to trick us into buying some of your 'new' company's concoctions and then polishing us all off. Berkshires instead of bullets eh?"

"I…I…I have absolutely no idea what you're talking about," blustered Lady Grubnot, her voice shaky, her fists clenched into balls of rage as she gazed in total bewilderment at the figures on the screen.

"Don't lie to us!" snapped Queen Sofia, sitting up in an armchair from a deathly slump and looking very much alive. "We know exactly what you have done!"

"You can't pin this on me!" shrieked Lady Grubnot. "You have no evidence. There's nothing traceable in those crisps. Your words would never hold up in a court of law."

"Hah!" shouted Princess Tabatha, rolling off a footstool she had been doubled over. "How do you know the poison is untraceable if it wasn't you that put it there?"

"It was a guess!" shouted Lady Grubnot. "I reasoned that whoever did this vile crime will have been clever enough to mask the flavour. I am blameless!"

"I stopped you poisoning one box of those Berkshire Crisps!" declared Emily, crawling out from behind the sofa and standing up. "But I didn't manage to stop you poisoning the other one. I don't know why the royal family members aren't dead but it's no thanks to you!"

"YOU!" screamed Lady Grubnot, spinning round. "How dare you address me in this way? Get out of my study and go back to your hovel, you revolting child. You'll be working the next six months of Sundays for your impertinence."

"Let the girl speak!" thundered King Harold, his voice so loud and forceful that Lady Grubnot jolted a couple of paces back from the screen.

"I worked out what you were up to," declared Emily, "and I resolved to stop your wicked plans. You are nothing but an evil, slave-driving tyrant and would-be royal murderer!"

"Hear, hear!" cried the royal family, who by now were all on their feet in rude health and applauding Emily's outburst.

"I said you have no proof of any murder plot, none of you!" shrieked Lady Grubnot.

"I think we do," replied Emily firmly. "You'd better watch the screen."

A staggered Lady Grubnot turned back to the screen, just in time to see a television-bearing trolley being pushed into the dining hall.

"HIM!" shrieked Lady Grubnot when she spied the boy pushing the trolley. "The urchin who works for Mr Faraday!"

"His name is Zak," snapped Emily, "and you're not fit to wipe his boots!"

"But how did he get in there?" demanded Lady Grubnot, her eyes twitching, her neck wobbling from side to side.

"My cousin Martin and I look like peas in a pod," replied Zak. "He works here so I just borrowed his pass. It was as easy as buying a packet of crisps."

"And it's a good thing you did!" laughed King Harold, patting Zak on the back. "If you hadn't have told us it was probably best not to eat those Berkshires just in case and recommended we pretended to play dead to get things moving, then our story would be quite, quite different."

Good for Zak, thought Emily. *He didn't take any chances with those crisps and he let the royals know exactly what was going on.*

Zak wheeled the TV to a place where everyone, both in the castle and in Lady Grubnot's study, could see it. Then he hooked up a camcorder to the TV and pressed play.

For a few seconds nothing happened, but then the screen flickered into life and showed the inside of a dark building, a few fingers of moonlight providing enough light to examine the place. The walls were made of wood and an old hayloft in the corner pointed to it being an ancient barn. Around the walls were racks of gleaming silver equipment, pipes and cables. After a few seconds the face of Arthur Proudfoot came into focus. He was looking directly at the camera with a smug smile on his face. He then started speaking.

"I can't wait to tell Lady Grubnot about you. She'll be tickled pink by the tale of a brain-empty mutt who sat by while I sabotaged her last high-end crisp rival. Seven crisp companies will have turned into one, just one. Think of that! Flooding, poisoning or electrical faults – we've heaped them all on her rivals and more! In days she'll have the entire market to herself. Her plan is brilliant but I assure you, my dog friend, she couldn't have done it without me. Yes, it was her idea and she's bankrolled it, but it's been me who has carried out the vital work at the crisp face, if you like. We're a team, you see – partners in crime and crisp-company destruction! Three cheers for industrial sabotage, Mr Silent Doggy!"

There was silence for a few moments as everyone took in the contents of the film. Proudfoot's face had gone totally white. His whole body seemed to have folded in on itself like an origami creation gone wrong.

"H-h-how did they get this footage?" gasped Lady Grubnot, her finger pointing at the screen like a shaky magician's wand. "How could you be caught on film saying those things, Proudfoot? How could you have been so STUPID?"

Zak put his fingers in his mouth and whistled, and in walked Shanita Ridge and Rufus. They nodded at the members of the royal family and went to stand next to Zak.

"This was our camera person," said Zak, crouching down and rubbing Rufus under the chin, while pointing at his circular dog collar.

Rufus greatly appreciated Zak's action in addition to the fact that there were so many new and interesting smells in the room.

"The Ridges had a tiny camera embedded in Rufus's collar," explained Zak. "They stood guard with him for a couple of nights but on the night the intruder broke in, they were asleep. Fortunately the camera did its job and filmed everything. The following morning they checked all of their wiring and discovered it had been tampered with by the same man caught on film. And that man is you, Mr Proudfoot."

"How clever!" cried Queen Sophia. "Rufus has just earned himself a big reward."

Suspecting that this human woman was saying something nice about him, Rufus padded over to her and let her stroke him. She grabbed some dog treats from a bowl normally reserved for the corgis and offered him several. He smelled them, licked them and then, with great delight, gobbled them all up.

"In addition to this proof about you breaking up the other crisp companies, I observed you making up the poison potion in your mixing tower," declared Emily.

Several royals gasped and shook their heads in total disbelief.

"That's ridiculous!" exploded Lady Grubnot. "No one has ever been in that tower but me."

"So how come I know you used chicken skin, oregano and odourless/tasteless/untraceable poison," said Emily.

This comment totally floored Lady Grubnot. Her mouth kept opening and closing like an out-of-control level crossing. But she pulled herself together and spoke out once more. "This is preposterous," she sneered. "It is the word of one small, disgusting child against the word of one of the world's greatest and most successful businesswomen. Who will the world believe?"

"They won't believe you," said another voice, as now Frank Ridge walked in.

"How many extra guests are you having today?" muttered Lady Grubnot.

"It just so happens that my sister is a prominent scientist," declared Frank. "The poison you added to the Berkshires, the poison you believe is so undetectable, only stays untraceable for a short time. She has tested both boxes of crisps and one has very clear traces of a deadly poison. Add to that the fact that my wife was waiting at Northurst Harbour and filmed Mr Proudfoot arriving with the boxes from Grubnot Island, boxes that you prepared, Lady Grubnot. Factor these in and suddenly, suddenly the case against you begins to stack up!"

Amazing! thought Emily, her spirits now so high she feared she might start floating. *Zak and the Ridges had all bases covered. Between us, we've nailed her!*

"Face it, Lady Grubnot," said Zak, looking at the screen with a determined glare. "It's all over."

"That is where you're wrong!" yelled Lady Grubnot.

And she reached for the emerald pendant round her neck.

Chapter Thirty-Four
The Emerald in Orbit

Emily had anticipated this move. She'd known that if things went against Lady Grubnot, and the Lady realised how central Emily was in the plot to bring her down, the woman could well resort to the most destructive strategy of all and blow up the entire island. That's why Emily had lashed Clemence's two stilts together and placed a small hook at one end.

As Lady Grubnot's finger went to press the emerald's activation switch, Emily thrust the hook under the Lady's pendant chain and quickly pushed up the stilt contraption. This resulted in the entire necklace with the emerald at its centre being lifted clean over Lady Grubnot's head. This sudden jolt made the emerald detach itself from the chain and go flying towards the ceiling of the study. For a moment it seemed to defy gravity, threatening to remain suspended up high, but a split second later it came crashing back down to earth.

Emily and Lady Grubnot both leapt up to grab it. But before either of their hands could reach it a tall figure out-jumped them and caught it first.

It was Clemence in his blue electrician's boiler suit (he'd been replacing a light bulb in the kitchen). He'd entered the room three seconds ago, just in time to see the falling emerald and Lady Grubnot's and Emily's desperate attempts to snatch it.

He held the gleaming green jewel in the palm of his left hand.

"HAND IT OVER THIS INSTANT!" roared Lady Grubnot, holding onto Emily's collar.

"DON'T DO IT, CLEMENCE!" begged Emily, pulling Lady Grubnot's shirtsleeves. "SHE'LL KILL US ALL!"

"GIVE IT TO ME NOW OR YOU WILL LOSE YOUR JOB AND BE TURFED OFF THIS ISLAND INTO A LIFE OF GUTTER-DWELLING POVERTY!" shrieked Lady Grubnot.

"NO, CLEMENCE! KEEP IT AWAY FROM HER!" beseeched Emily.

The two of them pushed and pulled each other, neither managing to defeat the other as Clemence viewed them with interest.

The gallery of characters on the screen stared in horror at the scene playing out before them, aware that an activation of the switch would destroy the island and all who were on it.

Clemence cleared his throat and, noticing the royal family were watching on the screen, gave them a quick bow and turned back to the warring combatants who were panting and hissing and growling at each other.

"I'm afraid I don't possess a hospital surgeon's gown and mask, nor am I a mortuary technician," he announced, "roles I would need to perform if this device was activated."

"PASS IT OVER, YOU IDIOT!" shouted Lady Grubnot.

"DON'T LET HER TOUCH IT!" shouted Emily.

"More importantly, however," went on Clemence, "it is clear in my mind that morality, fairness and the cause of non-violence do not require special attire or identifiable uniforms so I'm afraid, Lady Grubnot, that on this occasion, I will not acquiesce to your demands and the outcome will be as follows."

He held up the emerald and threw it with incredible force towards the fireplace, an act he had watched Lady Grubnot perfrom with plates and glasses and paperweights on many other occasions.

For a second Emily was terrified that on impact the activation switch be triggered, but the emerald splintered into hundreds of pieces that immediately became blackened by the roaring fire, and no explosions or fireworks occurred.

"HOW COULD YOU!" wailed Lady Grubnot.

"There's one thing I haven't yet told you," said Emily, the two of them still clasped in a raging battle.

"What is it, you evil child?"

"That film taken by the camera on Rufus's collar? If you think that's the only copy and that you could somehow get Mr Proudfoot to prise it away from the royals and destroy it, then think again."

"What are you talking about?" hissed Lady Grubnot.

"I got Zak to make multiple copies and post them to the world's press with an embargo on them being opened until the royals had seen it for themselves. When we sent the discs we included an invitation to wait at Northurst Harbour until a signal came for people to set off for Grubnot Island. Now that the royals have seen it, the press embargo has been lifted and the signal has been given. So that means you might be expecting some company shortly."

Lady Grubnot let out a horrified squeal, prised herself away from Emily and rushed over to the window, with Emily and Clemence close behind. There on the water were the first boats of a huge flotilla, all of them crashing over the water and making a beeline straight for Grubnot Island.

"I am RUINED!" screeched Lady Grubnot, but before Emily or Clemence could grab her and pin her down she'd sped out of the room. Emily raced after her, totally determined to stop her escaping.

Lady Grubnot hurtled down three flights of stairs, with Emily close behind and amazed at the pace of the Lady. Out onto the large tarmac square in front of the manor house burst Lady Grubnot, Emily racing in her wake, gritting her teeth and kicking her legs for maximum power.

The Lady swerved right and started racing down the path leading towards the northern side of the island and the rarely used north jetty. In fact, Emily had hardly ever been this way because there were no fruit trees or berry bushes and there were very few places to conceal yourself if you wanted to avoid the prying eyes of your boss.

I'm going to get her, thought Emily. *I'm going to stop her and wrestle her to the ground. Then I'm going to keep her there until the police make it here. She's finally going to get what's coming to her.*

But as the island fence came into view, Lady Grubnot scooped a couple of logs off the ground and chucked them behind her. One landed on the path, but the other hit the top of Emily's foot and, as well as causing her much pain, tripped her up and she fell heavily.

"Take that!" snarled the Lady, speeding on.

By the time Emily had got back to her feet, Lady Grubnot had put a decent distance between them and Emily's running was slower because of the pounding pain in her foot. So when Emily raced through the now open north jetty gate, she saw Lady Grubnot revving up the engine of an old-fashioned red-and-white pleasure boat.

That's the boat my mum described. The one she used to collect my family and the Walters all those years ago!

Emily hurtled forward, dead set on reaching her poisonous enemy, but just as she made it to the water's edge the boat started pulling away.

No. Please. No!

Emily considered trying to leap on board and continue the struggle on the boat but the gap between shoreline and vessel was already too great. She watched as Lady Grubnot issued her with a spiteful wave and stared helplessly as the boat picked up speed.

At this moment, Emily's feelings were of the mixed variety. *We've stopped her evil empire, we've freed my family, friends and me, and we've hopefully saved those other crisp companies. But we've also let her get away. She's left the island as a free woman when she should be behind bars. If the authorities aren't able to track her down then true justice will never be done.*

It was with this mingling of delirious joy and remorse about the escaped villain that Emily panted for a few moments before turning round and walking back up the path towards the manor house.

CHAPTER THIRTY-FIVE
MR PROUDFOOT'S HASTY EXIT

Back at Farham Castle, when Zak played the film captured by Rufus's doggy-cam in the Ridge's barn, Arthur Proudfoot was in serious danger of having a heart attack. He was furious with himself for conversing with a dog he had never met before and one that was obviously far cleverer than he'd given credit. Maybe the dog always wore a camera collar round his neck but Proudfoot somehow doubted it. That meant that he'd been set up. How could he, such a slick and devious operator, have suffered such a cruel and unexpected fate?

This though, couldn't be his main concern at the moment. He had just been exposed as a saboteur and prolific criminal, not to mention being caught up in a plan to KILL the royal family. If he didn't move quickly he would be facing a very long spell behind bars at several majesties' expense. His uncle had been in prison once and told him the food was horrible. Proudfoot loved his food. He wasn't going to settle for any swill.

So as Emily and the royals and Lady Grubnot exchanged un-pleasantries, Proudfoot slipped out of the room, hurried down the plushly carpeted stairs, and emerged into the afternoon sunlight. Two armed policemen who had not had the benefit of seeing the recently released film starring Proudfoot at the Ridges' place nodded at him jovially, while a security guard unlocked a gate for him to step out into the street. To his immense joy there was a taxi directly on the kerb in front of him.

He opened the back door and leapt in. "The nearest airport please," he said. "And I'll double your fare if you get me there in record time."

The driver was obliging, and the cab left the environs of the castle and drove at great speed down a series of twisting country roads. As he edged away from Farham Castle and a whole load of royal trouble, Proudfoot thought things over.

Lady Grubnot had offered him a huge sum of cash for his role in her plot and he was pretty sure now that he wouldn't be receiving any of this money. This was terribly disappointing and frightfully unjust as he'd played his part with aplomb and great skill. But she had paid him a few much smaller increments and he'd not spent these yet. So he had enough money to pay for this taxi ride and for a flight out of the country, plus a bit extra.

He would fly to Italy. Once there, he'd head down to the Calabria region where his old school friend Mac owned a small house at the end of a deserted track. Mac was also a criminal (he stole vases of flowers from people's houses and sold them in markets – the vases, not the flowers) and had been involved with the forces of law and order several times himself. But he'd recently told Proudfoot that his life of petty larceny was now over and that if Proudfoot ever needed a quiet place to rest his head then he should look him up. This would allow Proudfoot to lie low for a while, rent-free.

When all of the fuss had died down, Proudfoot would move on from Italy and seek out a great aunt who resided in Switzerland. She possessed a fair amount of money and he was sure he could wheedle some out of her. So long as he kept a low profile and wore a disguise, he was pretty confident he could avoid arrest and make a comfortable life in the Swiss Alps. Maybe he'd open a bar and rip-off gullible tourists.

Proudfoot was so busy contemplating his escape plan that he didn't focus on *where* the taxi was going. He was utterly surprised therefore when it pulled up in front of a large police station, whereupon two extremely beefy police officers pulled open the back door, dragged him out and handcuffed him.

"W…w…what's going on?" he spluttered.

"We received a tip-off," said one of the officers. "Someone said they'd be delivering a human package."

The officers proceeded to frogmarch the staggered Proudfoot inside the station. Luckily they didn't take much notice of the taxi driver as they wouldn't have been too keen on the fact that she was a fourteen-year-old girl whose vehicle displayed a shoddy handmade TAXI sign taped to the roof.

CHAPTER THIRTY-SIX
AN ENDING

By the time Emily emerged from the path, there was a huge amount of noise and excitement on the large tarmac square at the front of the manor house. A great mass of technical people were setting up television cameras, checking microphones, studying tablets, and texting on their mobiles, while their presenting colleagues were brushing their hair and smoothing down their beards, if they possessed them. And all the while the crowd was getting bigger. People were pouring up from the south jetty, eager to see what was going on.

It was Clemence who'd opened the large gate at the south jetty, allowing this amphibious media army to swarm onto the estate. Paul was there to meet him as Emily had asked and he was responsible for warning people to stick to the paths and refrain from touching the fence if they valued their lives. After opening the gate, Clemence had cordoned off an area on the tarmac where the news people could congregate, and had set up a lectern of the sort the President of the United States uses when he makes a speech. At first he was worried about what outfit he should wear as these tasks fell under different departments, but then it dawned on him that Lady Grubnot was gone and he entertained the rather wonderful prospect that from now on he'd be able to wear his casual inventing clothes whenever he wished (which would be pretty much all the time).

The news people had attached their microphones to the front of the lectern, giving it a brightly coloured, multi-headed alien-like appearance. They had been informed there would be a press conference and they were itching for it to begin.

A disc containing the Arthur Proudfoot footage had given the reporters an insight into Lady Grubnot's grand scheme of industrial sabotage, and the role of a heroic dog called Rufus. But the message that came with the disc said that the matter was also very closely linked to the royal family. Now, if there's one thing the press adore, it's a royal story, and this felt like it was going to be a big royal story, the mother or possibly grandmother of all royal stories, the royal story that would put all other royal stories into the shade.

Emily had expected some news people to arrive, but was staggered when she rounded the corner and saw the giant, excitable chaos in front of the manor house. As she approached, Clemence guided her to the lectern. She felt nerves thrashing around inside of her as the talking turned to whispers and the whispers turned to silence. There, staring at her, were her parents, her granddad and the three Walters, not to mention hundreds of other people holding gadgets and assorted pieces of equipment. A hush descended on those gathered. Lenses swivelled in her direction and microphones were switched on, all attention turned to this small girl.

Coughing nervously, she caught her parents' eyes, their expression ones of utter amazement. They were completely in the dark about what was going on, but certain that their daughter had played some central role in securing their apparent freedom.

When Emily tapped the nearest microphone an echoey *thud* reverberated across the tarmac.

"Ladies and gentlemen," she began, knowing that in the face of the dazzling lights and huge throng of people she'd have to explain things in the clearest way possible.

Cameras were steadied. Boom mikes were gripped.

"As you have all seen from the film captured by Rufus, Lady Wilhelmina Grubnot has been waging a war against her rivals in the top end of the crisp business. She and her henchman, Mr Arthur Proudfoot, used illegal methods to crush these other companies and erase them from the market."

Computer keys were tapped, pencils scribbled shorthand.

"When these companies had been destroyed and discredited, Mr Proudfoot tricked their distraught owners into selling them to her for ridiculously small prices."

Earpieces were adjusted. Sound recording levels were checked.

Emily felt the nerves starting to drift away as she got into her stride.

"But this was only part of her story. It wasn't ultimately the crisp companies she was after. She wanted to get them out of the way for a much darker purpose."

The huge mass of people stared at her with an intensity that was almost frightening. They sensed that this girl was about to drop a colossal bombshell.

"What she wanted to do was get *rid of the royal family*," went on Emily, "and by get rid of, I mean *kill*."

There were staggered gasps of shock. A couple of people dropped their laptops and one journalist from a big national newspaper bit a colleague in excitement. Kill the royal family. This wasn't a news story. This was a lava-fuelled volcanic eruption of the utmost ferocity.

"Lady Grubnot eliminated her competitors so that when the royals wanted to purchase some upmarket crisps there was just one company left for them to deal with: a new set-up going by the name of Berkshire Crisps."

Coughs were issued, ties were straightened.

"But Berkshires was a company secretly set up and run by Lady Grubnot. When the royals ordered some Berkshire Crisps – as Lady Grubnot knew they would – she produced a poisoned batch, put them in two Berkshires boxes and had them delivered to Farham Castle."

"NO!" blurted out several people in the media mass, one man drooling at the prospect of the pay rise he might get when he filed this story.

At that second Emily spotted a new group hurrying towards the giant gathering. It contained Zak, Cags, Shanita and Frank Ridge, and Rufus.

"Ifmybrilliantteamovereandmyfriend Paul–" everyone turned round to size up the new arrivals – "hadn't assisted me so superbly, we would now all be preparing for a great number of royal funerals."

"It's the camera dog!" someone shouted as the photographers started clicking away. Rufus barked obligingly. There were more fascinating smells here than he'd ever smelled before. He had a lot of investigating to do. Would there be extra doggy treats?

The media throng turned back to face Emily.

They had listened. They had digested the words. They had inputted them into their various contraptions. But they could contain themselves no longer and the questions started flying.

"How did you find out about her plan?"

"Who warned the royal family?"

"What kind of poison was it?"

"Where is Lady Grubnot?"

"What are you doing on Grubnot Island?"

Emily answered as many of these questions as possible, and told those gathered about how Lady Grubnot had captured her workforce and treated them, of the electrified fence and the unexploded bombs, about the manner in which she had managed to warn the Ridges and switched seasonings in the mixing tower, and the heroic way Clemence had caught the deadly airborne emerald and destroyed it.

At this last revelation Clemence blushed modestly while the camera lenses turned to him. As

Emily continued, more and more news people were still arriving: several European reporters had chartered helicopters and were now reaching the island, and one journalist who couldn't afford to hire a speedboat was heroically crashing through the water on a broken pedal boat. A rumour circulated that one junior reporter, so eager not to miss out on the action but devoid of a boat, had started swimming from Northurst Harbour (this turned out to be untrue but the story still appeared in several other newspapers). As the numbers continued to grow, Emily figured she'd be there for hours if she answered every question. So using a clever piece of misdirection (to divert their attention away from her), she calmly announced that the last sighting of Lady Grubnot had been at the north tip of the island, the north jetty.

"I saw her leave in a red-and-white boat," announced Emily. "She might still be on the water."

It was as if the starting gun for an Olympic hundred-metre sprint final had just been fired. Some people dropped their equipment and started a mad dash towards the north jetty, while others rushed back to their boats in an attempt to catch up with the villain of this outlandish story. Boy were they all going to sell a lot of papers and grab millions of viewers! And if anyone managed to track her down and possibly get an interview with her, well...they'd be garlanded with praise and media awards and could be the recipient of tantalising job offers from around the world, not to mention become a national hero for catching the would-be royal murderer.

This left Emily, her family, the Walters, the Ridges, Zak, Cags, Clemence, and of course Rufus alone in the sudden stillness. "It's all over," said Emily, walking towards them all. "We never have to work in that crisp-production room again. We're free."

Her parents and granddad hugged her tightly, as did Simon and Mel Walters. Paul repeatedly patted her on the back. The Ridges squeezed her shoulders. Rufus licked her shoes. Cags high-fived her.

They all pulled up chairs and formed a small circle.

"Clemence, can I ask you a question?" asked Emily.

He nodded.

"Did you see me that day when you were out with Lady Grubnot near the fence, the time she said she thought she'd spotted someone there?"

"I did indeed." Clemence nodded. "Lady Grubnot scared the living daylights out of me but I wasn't prepared to have you seen and punished."

"Thank you." Emily smiled.

Janet touched Clemence on the arm and he gave her a bow.

"I have a confession to make to everyone," announced Emily.

"This day gets more remarkable by the second," cried Bob.

All eyes were on this girl, this young child who had performed so heroically that day.

"What is it?" asked Janet.

"I love crisps," she replied.

"No!" thundered Bob. "We all hate them."

"I know, but I've only ever tasted one and I've waited my whole life to taste another. Working in that production room as well as being stultifyingly boring has also been so tough because wherever I look there are crisps."

"But how did this all start?" asked Monty, his eyes watery, his smile so radiant it looked like it had been superimposed on his face by a clever magazine editor. "I mean, you and Zak, Cags and the Ridges, not to mention Rufus, the Berkshires, Farham Castle. There's so much to take in."

"Have we got enough time?" asked Emily, listening to the yells and shouts of the press corps coming from the north jetty.

"You've got the rest of your lives." Zak beamed. "How about starting at the beginning? Why don't you tell them how we first met?"

So that's exactly what Emily did.

And in the days and weeks that followed, after telling her family and friends over the course of many hours about all the astounding things she'd been involved in, Emily *did* get plenty of chances to eat crisps. She tried a great many flavours, some of which she loved, some of which weren't to her taste. Except on these occasions she didn't need to produce them in Lady Grubnot's crisp-production room. She just did what everyone else does. She bought them from the local corner shop on the mainland.

www.jonnyzucker.co.uk

www.threeharespublishing.com

www.threeharespublishing/bookclub.com